Burden Stone

A Novel of the Camino de Santiago

by William Ray & Chris Danielson

Burden Stone
A Novel of the Camino de Santiago

ISBN-13: 978-0692099971
ISBN-10: 0692099972

Seaborne Books

Praise for *Burden Stone*

"It's a real page turner! I don't remember ever reading a book of 170 pages in one sitting! Once I started, I couldn't stop. At first glance I thought this was a travel story through a fascinating part of the world, but I soon began to identify with a couple looking for God's will in their lives … I have already invited my son to come with me on the Camino … Humor, tears, family, love, and a spiritual message underlying the whole story!"
- Rev. David Gooday, Anglican Cathedral of All Saints, Swaziland

****

"A riveting read which captures the imagination. In fact, I found myself travelling with the characters. Indeed I would love to hear the next installment."
- Robert Bailey, Pastor, Encounter Christian Fellowship, Victor Harbor, South Australia

****

"The writing is lively and well-paced, and the characters are thoroughly likable."
- J. L., literary agent

****

"I loved it and enjoyed every page! I was very touched by the story."

- Barbara Sumner

****

"It is such a lovely read … about somewhere I have been dying to go!"

- Frances Takis

****

"We all encounter rough patches on our journey through life but only after we hitchhike with Chris and Emilee on their challenging and eventful trip do we fully understand the potential blessings waiting for us along the way. *Burden Stone* is a special and inspiring story, a hike well worth experiencing."

- Don Keith, author of *Firing Point* (adapted for the major motion picture *Hunter Killer* starring Gerard Butler)

****

"Enjoyable and thought-provoking read, which helps answer the question: 'Can God still use me when everything seems to be going wrong?'"

- Rick Line

Dedications

William Ray
to
my daughters, Danielle and Rachel,
true pilgrims

Chris Danielson
to
my "fab four," Zackary, Dana, Jacob, and Hannah,
my heart companions for every step of the journey

MAP

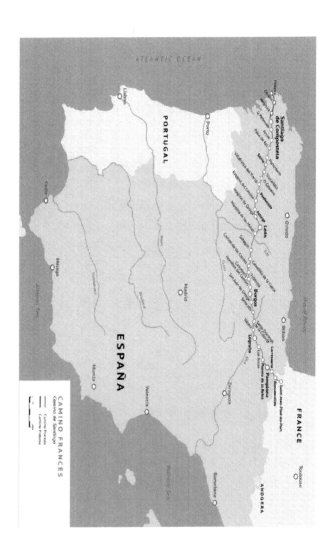

Inspired by a true story

TABLE OF CONTENTS

CHAPTER 1

A Long Way from Spain

Grand Rapids, Michigan – 4,000 miles from Spain

Emilee Danielson settled into the passenger seat of the little Camry in the pre-dawn darkness, sleepily tapping a packet of Organic Stevia into her coffee tumbler. She looked toward the driver's door, waiting.

Chris Danielson opened it and, practically creaking with drowsiness, dropped into the seat, the dome light briefly revealing signs of clutter about the car: empty water bottles and Tootsie Roll wrappers, grocery store coupons and a sunglasses case on the center console, a crushed box of Kleenex and CD cases wedged up against the back window, and on the back seat a sweater and a loose Bible tossed between two children's car seats. The smaller child's seat sported a pink polka dot Minnie Mouse dress pattern and the larger seat featured *Frozen's* Anna and Elsa.

Chris closed the door, inserted the key on the second try, started the car, and backed out of the driveway.

"Belt," Emilee said.

Chris strapped it on as he drove through the quiet neighborhood.

"Are you set with the Rush Hour Riddle?" Emilee asked.

"The Rush Hour Riddle?"

"Mm-hmm. It's your turn. Tell me you have something," Emilee said.

"I have something," Chris said, turning on to Lake Michigan Drive.

"Okay, let me hear it," Emilee said.

"There's a king, and sitting in front of the king are three goblets," Chris said.

Emilee nodded. "Okay, there's a king with three goblets in front of him."

Chris continued: "The first goblet is full. The second goblet is full. But the third goblet is empty."

"Okay, the first two goblets are full, and the third one is empty. Got it."

"What is the name of the king?" Chris said

"The name of the king...?" Emilee said slowly.

Chris reached for her tumbler, took a sip.

"I give up," Emilee said. "What's the name of the king?"

"Phil*up* the Third."

Emilee gave a short chuckle. Chris smiled.

"Turn on Jay's show. Wake us up," Chris said.

Emilee turned on the radio and For King and Country's upbeat "It's Not Over Yet" filled the car. Chris tapped the wheel. Emilee hummed and took a sip.

The sky lightened to gray as the traffic thickened.

"Did you send in the car insurance payment?" Emilee asked.

"I will. I'm thinking of shopping around. Did we ever set up the Visa for automatic payment?"

"I did. I think."

"The minimum, right?"

"Don't forget," Emilee said, "we're meeting with Anderson after the show."

"Oh, that's right." Chris laughed. "Maybe he wants to give us a raise."

"Mm-hmm."

Chris flinched and pumped the brakes as a silver F-150 cut in front of him. He let out a frustrated breath.

"I asked for one, you know?"

"What?" Emilee said.

"A raise. I asked for a raise."

She looked at him with surprise.

Chris shrugged. "I'm turning forty-five and make less than a son-in-law twenty years younger. Probably. Counting benefits and all."

"But together we do okay," Emilee said. "A raise would be nice."

Suddenly the notes of another song rang through the car, the chorus of TobyMac's "Love Broke Through," Emilee's ringtone for their daughter Dana. Emilee punched off the radio and dug out her cell phone.

"Early," Chris said.

"It's midmorning," Emilee said, finishing with an English accent, "across the pond."

She put the phone to her ear with a smile. "Hi, honey. Just driving to the station." Emilee listened.

"Okay, I'll—" Her phone pulsed. "Just got it. Talk later."

Emilee disconnected, lowered her phone, and began fingering the screen. "She sent us a video of Riley Pie!"

Chris smiled.

Emilee held the phone still as the video began. Chris tried to watch out of the corner of his eye but had to give up and content himself with listening closely.

"Ohh!" Emilee said.

Riley's little voice sounded out of the phone with a joyful laugh. "It's Pooh, Mommy!"

"How adorable," Emilee said.

"What? What are they doing?" Chris asked.

"Can I take him home?" Riley said.

"He's too big," Dana's voice answered. "We'll come visit him."

"Ohh!" Emilee said again.

"What? Where are they?" Chris said.

"Some store. Riley's sitting in a big stuffed Winnie-the-Pooh chair," Emilee said.

"Tomorrow, Mommy?" Riley said.

"We'll see," Dana said.

The video ended. Emilee's eyes filled with tears as she continued to look at the screen.

Chris glanced at the car seats in his rearview mirror. "That reminds me. I guess I can move those out of here."

"They'll be coming for Christmas, maybe even

Thanksgiving," Emilee said.

Chris smiled humorously. "You're right—that will give me only six or seven months to put them back in."

Emilee didn't answer. She lowered the phone and looked straight ahead.

Chris glanced at her, saw that he should drop it.

"Aren't there enough bases in America?" Emilee said.

"Christmas will be here before you know it," Chris said.

He slowed and turned into the radio station parking lot under a sign that read: "WGRT. The music is our message."

CHAPTER 2

Going Commercial

"Good show, Emilee," the receptionist said.

"Thanks, Rene." Emilee had stopped by Rene's U-shaped desk in the lobby to wait for Chris. "I'll have to show you the cutest video when I get a chance," Emilee said.

Emilee looked down the hall for Chris and saw him in the DJ lounge talking and laughing with the sound engineer, Bo. Beyond them, on the other side of the soundproof window, the midday host settled into his headphones at the microphone desk.

The phone rang, and Rene answered in her headset: "WGRT, where the music is our message. How can I help you?"

Chris walked down the hall with a bounce in his step, as usual after a show. He circled Rene's desk in the direction of the lobby doors, looking curiously at Emilee. "Ready?" he said.

"Our meeting with Anderson," Emilee said.

"Oh, right," Chris said.

Anderson's office was just a few feet off the lobby down another hall. The door, with its Station Manager sign, was ajar, and Chris and Emilee entered to find Anderson standing behind his desk, his laptop on the desk in front of him, lightly playing the station channel, a Big Daddy Weave song. Anderson, at thirty years old, was somewhat younger than Chris, but the two were good friends and took turns leading the men's Bible Study at the station.

Also present, and drawing curious and slightly anxious looks from Chris and Emilee, was Mr. Page, the station owner. He was only thirty-five years old, but ran a professional station. He stood beside the desk, rocking on the balls of his feet.

"Sorry we're late," Chris said. "I got to talking. We didn't know you'd be here, Mr. Page." Chris shook his hand, then joked awkwardly, "The Nielsens aren't out yet, are they?"

"How is Kate?" Emilee asked.

"Counting the days," Mr. Page said. "They'll induce this one if she goes to term."

Anderson tapped his keyboard, muting the song. "Good show, you guys," he said quietly. "As always."

"Sit down, folks," Mr. Page said.

They all took chairs, Mr. Page sitting on the edge of his.

"I'm no minister," Mr. Page said, "but I like to think I'm in the Lord's work. That's why I bought out this radio station from my dad."

"Certainly you are," Chris said.

Emilee nodded.

Mr. Page continued, "But I have to apply the business principles I've learned—from an expensive masters and, more importantly, experience—to the running of the station. I've made the decision to go commercial, to start taking paid ads."

"Oh," Chris said.

"Our Give-A-Thons are falling short. And they're tough on the talent."

"We do get to talk to a lot of wonderful people," Emilee said.

"But I can't say I look forward to those weeks," Chris said. "Commercial, huh? As long as the ads and businesses are in good taste—family-friendly—I guess we'd go along. Right, Em?"

"I'm also letting our street team go. Our DJs will do the remotes," Mr. Page said.

"You're letting Robyn go?" Emilee said.

Mr. Page nodded. Anderson looked at his desk.

"Listeners and sponsors want the DJs," Mr. Page said.

"I've always liked remotes," Chris said.

"And we're going automated overnight," Mr. Page said. "Jay's young and fresh and swims like a fish in the social media pool, so we're keeping him—"

"Good," Chris said.

"—and giving him the morning show."

Chris and Emilee stared at him, confused. Anderson continued to look at his desk.

"It's not just a business decision," Mr. Page said. "I've worked out some deals with local schools for live remotes with Jay. After school, registration week, special events. We'll reach a lot of kids."

"We do the morning show," Chris said. "In fact, I

distinctly remember walking out of the broadcast studio just a few minutes ago after polishing off another beauty."

"I have to let you go. You do a fine show, and the ratings aren't bad, but I have to pay you both."

"You can keep Chris on," Emilee said. "I can quit, or you can cut my salary, or—"

"No, Em. No way," Chris said.

"He's right. You're a team show," Mr. Page said. "All your bits—the Rush Hour Riddle, Devotions in Motion, the groaner jokes—you do together. And you do them well. But going commercial, we're going to have enough gab. People tune in for the music."

Chris ran his fingers through his hair, looked at Anderson. "So that's a 'No' on the raise?"

"I'm real sorry, you guys," Anderson said.

"You have a contract on a book?" Mr. Page said.

Chris brightened. "*Bible Sidekick*. I'm putting the finishing touches on it. A few more weeks and it goes to the publisher."

"We'll invite you back for an interview or two to promote it," Mr. Page said. "But this morning was your last show. You know how it goes."

CHAPTER 3

When It Rains...

Chris and Emilee, sitting with quiet and drained faces in the Camry, pulled up at the Starbucks drive-thru window. The teenage barista opened the window.

"Hi! So that's one Java Chip Fra—"

"Make that Java Chip a venti," Chris said.

"Chris," Emilee said.

"You don't get fired every day," Chris said.

"Could you add some extra vanilla to the latte?" Emilee said. "And some whip cream?"

"Sure!" the barista said.

Chris handed her his credit card and the drive-thru window closed.

"Here comes that homeless guy," Emilee said.

"That's Mystic Jimmy," Chris said.

A tall, coat rack-thin man crossed toward them from the street corner. He was at least sixty-five years old but walked with a spry step and bright, blue, saucer-wide eyes that resonated intensity. His long gray hair and a matching beard were streaked with strands of Scottish red.

"He's not homeless," Chris said. "Well, yes, he doesn't have a home. But he travels around preaching. Styles himself something of a prophet, definitely the Old Testament variety. But I think he's all there, mostly."

"You know him?" Emilee said.

"We've talked a few times."

Jimmy walked around the front of the car, approached Chris' window, and bent his tall frame to look inside, seemingly oblivious to the drive-thru window behind him and the other vehicles waiting in line behind the Camry. "Phil*up* the Third—ha, ha!" Jimmy said—loudly, as always. He leaned a little closer, glaring at Emilee. "I like your voice," he said, then to Chris: "Read my latest message? I gave you a copy, right?"

The barista opened the drive-thru window and politely tapped Jimmy on the shoulder. "Sir? Excuse me, sir."

Jimmy didn't notice her tap, or the honk from one of the vehicles behind the Camry.

"America must return to God!" Jimmy said. "That's what it's about."

Chris nodded.

"Can we buy you a drink, Mystic Jimmy?" Emilee said.

Chris gave her a quick, mortified look.

"Who?" Jimmy said. "*Mystic* Jimmy? Hey, I like that—and you."

Emilee passed a five dollar bill to him. Jimmy turned to face the barista. He said, "A latte. Venti. Hot. Quad shot. Eight pump vanilla. Foam. Extra hot." As Jimmy ordered, he took their drinks from the barista and passed them to Chris, spilling some in the process.

Two more honks issued from the cars behind them.

Jimmy looked at Chris. "Hey, I think there's a line forming. You better get going." Jimmy turned to the clerk. "I'll pick mine up inside."

Chris pulled forward but Jimmy suddenly turned and banged on the roof. Chris hit the brakes and frowned at him.

"One more thing," Jimmy said. "You're supposed to go in there." He pointed at the strip mall on the opposite corner of the intersection.

"The tanning salon?" Chris said.

"No, the travel agency."

"Why?"

"A flock of birds settled on that roof just as you drove up. It was a sign. They were facing east."

Chris and Emilee exchanged a look, Chris mouthing, "Mystic."

"The last thing we can afford right now is a trip, Jimmy."

But Jimmy had already turned back to the barista. "Add another pump of syrup," he said.

More honks. Jimmy gave a friendly wave to the honkers and walked around the front of the store. Chris drove off.

Chris pulled into their driveway, turned the key, and took out his cell phone. "You go ahead," he said to Emilee. "I'm going to call the publisher. I need a warm fuzzy."

"I'll let Harley out," Emilee said.

She climbed out and closed the door.

Judy answered: "This is Impact. Judy speaking."

"Judy. Chris Danielson."

"Chris! You have that manuscript for me?"

"I'm a couple months behind schedule, Judy, but it's coming. That all right?"

"Well, we're anxious to get it for the fall cycle...."

"I'm kind of down, Judy. We just got canned."

"What?"

"WGRT just let us go."

"Why?"

"Something tells me it's because I'm turning forty-five."

There was silence on the other end of the line. "You there?" Chris said.

"Do you have another station lined up?" she asked.

"It was a total shock to us," Chris said.

"Chris, your contract with Impact for—what's your book's title?"

"*Bible Sidekick*."

"Your contract is based on your radio job," Judy said.

"It's still the same book. Don't you like it?"

"I haven't read it," she said.

"Really?" Chris said.

"Don't sound hurt," she said. "We sign authors based on their platform, their connection to a wide audience who can buy their books. Oh, we checked your bona fides—we don't want to promote a cult—but the contract stipulates your position as a radio host. Same for the advance."

"This is no warm fuzzy, Judy," Chris said.

"Nor on my side. I was counting on you, Chris. I'll give you a month to land on your feet at a station with an equivalent audience—at least. I hope it works out, but without the platform there's no reason to send me the manuscript."

Chris noticed Emilee coming out the front door, looking upset.

"Understand, Chris?" Judy said.

"I understand. A job and a manuscript within the month. Look, Judy, I gotta go."

Chris rolled down his window as Emilee approached.

"Chris, you forgot to let Harley back in this morning," she said. "I don't know where he's crawled off to."

Chris sighed, started the car. "I'll go try to find him."

"What did Judy say?"

Chris just shook his head as he backed out of the driveway.

CHAPTER 4

Just a Sinner

"—yes, a few days ago, our resume and MP3 files of the show. Did they come through?" Chris held the phone to his ear as he paced around his desk, on the corner of which curled a fat, balding cat—Harley. Chris was dressed as he would for work—khakis, shirt and sweater, penny loafers—but it had been a week since their firing. The curtains were drawn back on a bright morning and a yard that needed mowing. "Hey, listen. I could drive on over to Ann Arbor, no problem, get a cup of coffee—"

Chris' pacing slowed as he continued to listen.

"Right," he said. "I understand."

Chris sat at his desk, wearing blue jeans and a Michigan State sweatshirt, the phone to his ear, his eyes closed. He nodded in resignation. "I understand. Thanks." He disconnected, reached for a sticky note, and punched in the number written on it.

Chris, wearing gardening shorts, a grass-stained t-shirt, and a #3 Dale Earnhardt hat, was passing through the kitchen on his way to the backdoor—the lawnmower awaited—when he heard his laptop chime. He retraced his steps to his office, sat at the desk in front of the open laptop and tapped the touchpad.

Emilee followed, stopping in the door with a hopeful look.

Chris took a deep breath and read the email out loud: "'Dear Mr. and Mrs. Danielson'—etc., etc.— 'Thank you for your interest' —etc.—'Unfortunately, we have recently filled the positions for which you applied....'" His voice trailed off and he slumped in the chair. Emilee lowered her head and turned away.

Chris sat in the arm chair opposite his desk, listening lethargically to the phone at his ear, watching Harley, who, perched on the windowsill behind his desk, licked stupidly at the raindrops falling on the other side of the window.

Chris, dressed again in his khakis, shirt and vest, and loafers, walked briskly back and forth in front of his desk, a forced smile on his face as he spoke earnestly into the phone: "The afternoon show will also work. We've always been able to grow an audience, we're proud of that—grateful. We—" Chris listened. "Yes, twenty years, the last twelve here in—" Chris listened, forced a laugh. "We can get used to some humidity. If you—"

Chris' pacing came to a stop. He put a hand over his eyes and listened.

"Can I send you any more information? A recording from one of our remotes? Maybe a—"

Chris listened.

"Yeah. I understand. Bye."

Chris disconnected, leaned back against his desk, and closed his eyes. Then he turned, picked up his keys off the desk, and exited the office. "I'm going out, Em," he called.

Chris, by default, had the radio stationed tuned to WGRT as he drove. He did ok as the songs played, but when the announcer came on with the logo, "WGRT. The music is our message," it hurt too much, and he frowned and turned it off.

He had intended to drive to their church to see if he could catch a few minutes with the pastor, but instead he headed for Starbucks and got Pastor Tyler on the phone—a lucky break; the man was always busy.

"We could use your prayers, Pastor," Chris said as he waited for his drink at the Starbucks drive-thru window.

"You bet, Chris. It's a shame about your job. We had a number of people come to our church from your show."

"If nothing else turns up soon, is the Family Ministry position still open for me?"

Pastor Tyler did not answer right away, but then he said, "It's not filled yet."

"Thanks, Tyler," Chris said. "See you Sunday."

Chris took his Frappuccino from the barista—the same one who had served them on the day they were fired—and pulled forward; but he slowed, almost to a stop, when his eyes locked on the travel agency in the strip mall on the opposite corner, which Mystic Jimmy had pointed out to them. The travel agency had a corny name painted in tropical colors on its window front: "Grand RAPIDs TOURS & TRAVEL."

"A flock of birds settled on that roof just as you drove up," Mystic Jimmy had said.

Chris chuckled at the memory. "No birds today."

But when he pulled out of the Starbucks' parking lot, he put on his blinker, crossed a couple lanes, and turned into the strip mall. It was just the travel agency that appealed to him; maybe they could take a cheap trip somewhere. He climbed out of the Camry with his Frappuccino, stepped onto the sidewalk, and entered the shop.

It was a small agency with only one desk, at which sat a young woman with short wavy black hair across from a frowning, brawny-backed Catholic priest in full clerical collar.

"I'll be with you in a moment, sir," the young woman said.

"No problem," Chris said. He thumbed through the brochure rack as the agent chattered and the priest grunted one-word answers. The brochures ranged from the Bahamas and Hawaii to "Mackinac Island State Park" and the "Henry Ford Museum." Chris focused on the latter—all they could afford.

"I've heard great things about this walk, Father," the agent said, "usually from transplanted Europeans.

Wonderful scenery, quaint hostels, and of course the exercise—almost 500 miles along the main route!"

"Pilgrimage," the priest said gruffly.

"Sounds romantic—and spiritual, of course," the agent said. "The Camino de Santiago—what is that in English?"

"The Way of Saint James. The pilgrimage leads to the shrine where the Apostle's bones are said to be buried," the priest explained.

"And this is your third time to take the walk. You must really love it." She paused. "Aren't you excited?"

"I've never been more excited about anything in my entire life," the priest answered, his voice gruff and monotone.

At the sound of it Chris looked up, expecting sarcasm on the priest's face. But he wore the same frown and seemed to have meant every word.

"That's a lie," the priest continued. "I was more excited about my first deployment with the Corps."

Chris noticed the priest's bristly crew cut, and a tattoo of an M16 assault rifle on the left side of his neck, a couple inches above the collar.

"You're all set, Father," the agent said.

He took the packet she handed him, grunted a thank you, and stood, unfolding a six-foot-four frame complete with linebacker shoulders and a flat stomach. He walked toward Chris, revealing ink on the right side of his neck as well: discarded bullet cartridges flying through the air, as though just fired by the M16 on the other side of the neck.

Chris, one who'd never met a stranger, smiled at him. "You must have been the meanest, baddest dude in your seminary," he said.

The priest stopped and looked at Chris. "I was."

Christ pointed at the tattoos on the priest's neck. "The Marines allow those?"

"No, but a kid can forget a lot of things on a three-day leave. And remember others. You can't hide from the Almighty."

"So this pilgrimage—what's the point?" Chris asked.

"The Camino de Santiago? For many—for the devout since the Middle Ages—it's a journey of penance, to atone for guilt. For others a retreat from the world to find God. For others a grueling adventure across Spain, from the Pyrenees in the east to the city of Santiago in the west—almost to the Atlantic."

Chris again considered the priest's powerful frame. "500 miles. Can ordinary humans make it?" Chris asked.

"I'm taking a group of thirty on this tour. I expect twenty or twenty-one to drop out along the way. Only a few make it to the cross."

"The cross?"

"The Cruz de Ferro toward the end of the journey, where the burden stones are laid down."

Chris shook his head. "I don't understand."

The priest took an impatient breath. "Pilgrims write

their burdens—sins, needs, prayer requests, sufferings—on stones at the beginning of the journey and offer them at the foot of the cross on the way. Most of my parishioners will have handed their stones off to me well before then."

"A pilgrimage. Wow. Do you have to be Catholic?"

"Just a sinner," the priest said.

Chris smiled humorously. "If I did it, can you guarantee I'll look like you on the other side?"

The priest glanced at Chris' drink, and cracked half of a half-smile, just the very corner of his mouth nudging upward. "No, you won't look like me. Peace, brother."

When Chris returned home, entering the living room from the garage—he had finally had enough time to clear out space in it for the Camry, one of Emilee's "Unemployed Honey-Do" tasks for him—he was tapping a travel agency brochure in his palm and smiling.

Emilee was cooling down on her Pilates mat.

"Good news?" she said. She rose from the mat and grabbed her towel.

"You believe in seeking God?" Chris asked.

She glanced at her Bible lying open near the Pilates mat. "Yes."

"And you're always saying I need more exercise?"

"Both of us," she said.

"And we've always wanted to travel."

"What is this?" Emilee asked.

Chris held up the brochure and walked toward the kitchen. "Come take a look."

They sat at the kitchen table with the brochure spread between them, the light over the table flashing off its glossy pages. It had grown dark outside the kitchen windows.

"It's about the only kind of trip we can afford," Chris said. "The agent said there are cheap places, called *albergues*, every few miles for the pilgrims."

Emilee sat back, looked at him. "Don't we need to look for a job?"

"I know it doesn't make much practical sense—people will say we're crazy—but we'll just be stepping out on faith. We won't rush, won't over-plan, but just walk and pray and maybe journal and ask God to speak to us. 'What's next, Lord? Why has everything dried up? Haven't we served you?'" He could not prevent a note of bitterness from entering his tone.

Emilee lowered her eyes. "Like the pastor says, the Christian life can't be all mountaintop experiences—high points—there are often valleys in-between."

Chris took her hands. "Emilee, every door I've knocked on is closed, slammed shut. We have no prospects. We're running out of money. I don't know what to do. Let's just go somewhere there are no distractions and see if we can hear from God." He paused. "We'll fly in through England. Stay a few days."

Emilee jumped up. "I'll go call Dana!"

Chris held on to her hands. "Wait. So you'll go?"

"Of course."

Chris smiled smugly at her.

"What?" she said.

"That was my big gun—'We'll fly in through England'—I was saving it for last."

Emilee laughed at him as she turned away.

"What's so funny?" he said.

Emilee laughed to herself as she went down the hall. "Nothing, honey."

CHAPTER 5

Sometimes/Sometimes Not

Ten days later—Chris had been serious about not over-planning—they rode in the middle seat of the blue Super Shuttle van on their way to the Gerald R. Ford International Airport, their carry-ons beside them, no other passengers in the van. They were holding hands and smiling at the adventure ahead of them.

Their route took them past the intersection with the Starbucks on one corner and the strip mall with Grand RAPIDs TOURS & TRAVEL on the opposite corner.

"It looks like Mystic Jimmy is back," Emilee said.

"Driver, do you mind pulling into that parking lot for a minute?"

The driver, a handsome black kid without a whisker on his face, shrugged. "No other pickups this morning." He turned into the Starbucks lot.

Chris slid the door open. "Jimmy! Hey, Jimmy, over here."

Jimmy was standing near the corner, with cars rushing by, and it took him a moment to realize he was being called. Then he turned and walked over to the van. He was carrying a stack of papers.

"Hey, I don't hear you anymore," Jimmy said.

"We got canned, but we're off to follow the birds," Chris said.

"What?" Jimmy said.

"You know, the birds you saw land on the travel agency roof. You said they were a sign. That we were supposed to go in there. Well, I did, and one thing led to another, and, long story short, that's why we're headed to the airport—to walk across Spain on a pilgrimage."

"On our last dollar," Emilee added.

"Hmm," Jimmy said. He handed Chris one of his papers. "My new message."

"Say, Jimmy," Chris said. "These signs of yours—do they always work out?"

Jimmy considered this. "Sometimes," he said. "Sometimes not."

He returned to the corner. Chris and Emilee stared after him for a few seconds. Slowly, Chris slid the door closed.

"'Sometimes. Sometimes not'?" Emilee said.

Chris ran his fingers through his hair.

The driver looked at Chris in the rearview mirror. "You're spending your last dollar on a trip to Europe because some birds landed on a building?" the driver said.

"Just drive," Chris said.

CHAPTER 6

What Is This *Musique?*

The Camino de Santiago is a 500-mile journey across Spain, but it begins in France—at least, the pilgrimage's most popular route, known as the Camino Francés, does—in the little tourist town of Saint-Jean-Pied-de-Port in the foothills of the French Pyrenees, ten steep miles from the Spanish border.

Chris and Emilee's bus put them out on the cobbled streets of this mountain village at eight o'clock on a Friday night. They had intended to travel all the way by rail. After a too-short visit with Dana, Michael, and the granddaughters (it was *especially* too short with the granddaughters) in their pretty English home outside Lakenheath Air Force Base, near Cambridge, they had hopped the bullet train from London to Paris, continued south on Rail Europe to Bordeaux, and then farther south and west to Bayonne on the Bay of Biscay, where they were to switch lines one more time for the last leg of the journey to Saint Jean. But a work stoppage of some sort—Chris and Emilee did not understand the French words on the picketers' signs—required authorities to herd passengers onto buses instead. And by the time Chris and Emilee found a bus with empty seats and that bus climbed into the foothills of the Pyrenees, a six-hour trip had taken twelve.

Chris and Emilee collected their backpacks, the sum

of their "luggage" for the next five or so weeks on the trail, and started down *Rue de la Citadelle* in search of a hotel.

But in the first lobby they entered, the clerk across the counter shook her head and said to Chris, "I am sorry, *monsieur, mais nous n'avons pas de chambres*—no vacancy," and she pointed at the letter board sign on the wall behind her, which declared, "*Complet*."

And so it went from one quaint little *maison* to another, until they stopped on the sidewalk and read with resignation the same word on signs outside the remaining hotels on the street: "*Complet*."

"Maybe we should rethink our prohibition against planning," Emilee said.

"Let's get something to eat," Chris said.

They found a corner café and asked for one of the small round tables on the patio. It was a perfect late summer night, the mountain air cool and sweet. Moths circled the lights at the corner behind them.

The waiter placed their order, sandwiches and chips, in front of them and asked, "Can I get you anything else?"

"Got any rooms?" Chris joked. "The train from Bayonne was down and we got the last bus here."

"It is the summer season yet, *monsieur*," the waiter said. "Saint-Jean-Pied-de-Port is packed with tourists and"—he nodded at their backpacks—"pilgrims like yourself."

A busboy, who was walking by with a handful of

plates, stopped. "*Les Américains* need a room?" he said. "I heard customers—*Maison Melanie et Robert*, around the corner, had a last-minute cancellation."

Chris jumped up, grabbing their packs. "I'll run and get the room. Get it to go, Emilee."

The *Maison Melanie et Robert* was a converted house with a small lobby lit by a hazy yellow light on the counter, in front of which Chris and Emilee stood waiting. Emilee held a grease-stained paper sack and Chris read an entry in a pilgrim's guidebook and grumbled to himself.

The proprietor, Melanie, emerged from the staircase. She was a thin, hard-eyed woman, perhaps forty-five years old, with long brown hair streaking gray. She held a cell phone at her side. "The room is ready," she said with a heavy French accent. "*Suivez-moi.*" She turned to lead the way up the stairs, but Chris spoke.

"The guidebook says €50, not €60, for your place," he said. "This is the *Maison Melanie et Robert*, isn't it?"

Melanie stopped on the stairs, turned, and looked at Chris. "Obviously, the guidebook is old, *monsieur. Suivez-moi, s'il vous plaît.* The third floor."

They followed her up the enclosed staircase. Chris brought up the rear, wearing his backpack and carrying Emilee's, who, still holding the greasy sack, attempted to dial her cell phone with the other hand. "I told Dana

I'd call when we got in," Emilee said.

They exited the staircase at the third floor and followed Melanie down the narrow hall, when music suddenly played from Emilee's phone. Melanie turned to look.

"Sorry, I pressed the wrong—" Emilee fumbled with the phone trying to get the song to stop.

The song was Needtobreathe's "Keep Your Eyes Open," a stirring and hopeful rock anthem. Emilee tucked the paper sack under her arm and thumbed at the screen, but the song continued to play as they made their way down the hall. Melanie continued to stare over her shoulder until she reached the last door in the hall, and the music stopped.

"I hope I didn't wake anybody," Emilee said.

"What is this *musique?*" Melanie asked her.

"Needtobreathe, a Christian band," Emilee said.

Melanie made a disbelieving face. "Church *musique?*"

"Contemporary Christian. It's what we played. We're DJs."

"Where do I find it?" Melanie said.

"Anywhere. Any streaming—"

Melanie shook her head. "*Mais je ne sais pas*—I don't know what to look for, who to trust. And I cannot afford...."

Emilee pointed at Melanie's phone, which she still held at her side. "May I?"

Melanie handed her the phone and watched,

suspiciously, as Emilee tapped the screen.

"This will connect you to"—Emilee cast a sheepish glance at Chris—"our old station's network."

Chris frowned.

Tenth Avenue North's "You Are More" began to play on Melanie's phone.

"There you are," Emilee said.

Melanie took the phone back and listened with wonder.

"He must hear this," she said quietly, with emotion.

She opened the door and, without entering, reached inside and flipped on the light. "*Bonne nuit*," she said and walked away down the hall.

Chris and Emilee entered, looked around at the simple set of furniture—a double bed with a floral quilt, a small dresser and mirror, an old wooden chair—and Chris set their backpacks on the floor. Emilee put a finger to her nose. Chris made a face.

"What's that?" Chris said.

"I think I heard a toilet flush downstairs," Emilee said. "Can we open the window?"

Chris pulled back the curtain and raised the pane. "It's out here too," he said. "Maybe a backed-up septic. Should I say something?"

"Do we have a Plan B?" Emilee said.

"I'm going to say something."

Chris exited the room, leaving the door half-open. Emilee sat on the bed (its slats creaked), dialed Dana's number, and put the phone to her ear. She raised a finger to her nose again as she waited. The call went to voice mail.

Dana's voice: "Hi, this is Dana and Michael."

Riley's voice, filled with a four-year-old's excitement: "This is Riley!"

Two-year-old Quinner's little voice: "I'm Quinner."

Dana again: "Please leave a message."

Beep.

"We're in. Already miss you," Emilee said.

Chris returned. "No sign of her. Perhaps it's best. Like you said, we have no Plan B."

"We barely have a Plan A, honey."

CHAPTER 7

Where's Your Faith?

When Chris and Emilee stepped out of the front door of the *Maison Melanie et Robert* the next morning, carrying their backpacks, squinting sleepily against the rising sun, Melanie drove up in a jeep with the top down and stopped in the street. Somehow, she looked ten years younger. A bright red band gathered her long hair neatly behind her neck, her eyes were liquid brown, and she smiled at them.

"Oh, you are leaving?" she said. "Off on pilgrimage? But you must get your *credencial* at the Pilgrim Friends Office, *oui?* I will drive you."

Chris and Emilee looked at each other and walked toward the jeep.

They stashed their packs up front and sat in the backseat for the short drive through town. Fresh air blew pleasantly in their faces. Melanie was surprisingly talkative, and they leaned forward to try to understand her half-French, half-English statements, spoken in an enthusiastic rush. At the same time, they attempted to take in the town for the first time in daylight—a town of narrow cobblestone streets, white walls, and red roofs. Tourists ambled between gift shops and sidewalk cafés, taking pictures with cell phones, leading dogs on leashes, rubbing sunscreen on children's faces. Pilgrims were apparent too, identifiable by their backpacks and walking sticks, and many walked in the direction Melanie was driving.

"He listened to *la musique de Dieu* all night long," Melanie said.

She glanced over her shoulder to make sure Chris and Emilee understood. They weren't sure they did, but nodded—she spoke with such hope.

"*Il pleurait et,* er"—she took her hands off the wheel briefly, pressing them together in a prayer gesture—"*le Notre Père.* He has always been a disciple of Voltaire. *Candide.* But *le Notre Père, le Notre Père.*"

She came to a stop outside a brick archway out of which a line of pilgrims-to-be stretched, men and women of all ages, as well as a spattering of teens and a couple children.

"*Les Amis du Chemin de Saint Jacques,*" Melanie said. "That is, the Pilgrim Friends Office."

She climbed out with them, waited for Chris to grab the packs, and walked with them toward the line.

"Thank you for the ride," Emilee said.

"Yes, thanks," Chris said.

Melanie waved her hand. "You will walk plenty. *Bien,* the line is already moving."

And indeed the line shuffled forward as they reached the back of it. The line extended through the archway into the Pilgrim Friends Office, whose door was wide open. Melanie smiled and waved at someone inside the office. Then she turned to Chris and Emilee.

"*Merci. Au revoir.*" She turned and walked toward her jeep.

"Is that the same woman who rented us a stinky room last night?" Chris said.

The line advanced swiftly enough, and within fifteen minutes they sat with other pilgrims in plastic chairs in front of a long narrow table across from clerks assisting them in French, Spanish, and accented English. The office contained the usual business equipment—phones, letter trays, file cabinets, laptops, pens—as well as pilgrimage-specific items—an embroidered tapestry of a medieval pilgrim on the far wall, hiking charts, posters, and maps. A low hum of friendly conversation filled the office.

A French clerk, whose nametag identified as Marcel, passed papers across the table to Chris and Emilee. "These are your official *credenciales*—your pilgrim passports, if you will—which will be stamped at each station along the Camino. Starting here." The *credenciales* unfolded like brochures, each page divided into blank squares for stamps, the first of which the clerk now applied, lifting the wood-handled stamp from its ink pad and impressing the words "Saint-Jean-Pied-de-Port" in an oval, forest-green seal on square one. The front page of the passport contained an image of a scallop shell and the back page a place for information: name, country of origin, date (separate blanks for the beginning and end dates of the pilgrimage), and the locale from which the pilgrim was departing (a label reading "St-Jean-Pied-de-Port" had already been stuck here).

"You must also present them at the *albergues*," he said, "the inexpensive pilgrim hostels along the route, in order to receive a bed. And finally you will present them in Santiago as proof you have walked the whole way and deserve the *Compostela*."

"The *Compostela?*" Chris said.

"A diploma of sorts, signifying you have completed the Way. And this"—he unfolded a glossy map on the table—"this map breaks the Camino into thirty-four stages which can, ideally, be walked in about one day each. It tells the kilometers between each stage and gives the elevations. Your guidebook will do the same. The first stage is generally considered the most trying, as you are crossing the Pyrenees Mountains from France into Spain by the Napoleon Route—the pass he used to invade Spain."

"But pilgrims come in peace, eh?" The comment came from the chair beside Chris, where a young man with thick dark hair, swarthy skin, and porcelain-white teeth sat with his long legs crossed. He smiled.

"These two pilgrims do," Chris said.

The young man nodded politely at Emilee. "Of course, I had no doubt about *la bella donna*."

"Ah, *un Italien*," the French clerk said.

The handsome young man nodded.

Chris   reached   and   shook   his   hand.   "Chris

47

Danielson."

"Ah, you are *Americano*. I am Gino."

A grandmotherly clerk returned to the office from the back room and sat in the chair across from Gino. "I'm sorry for the interruption, Mr. Genovese, but I nearly forgot his birthday and that won't do—you know how important family is...."

She continued her conversation with Gino as Chris turned back to their clerk.

"First-timers," the clerk said, "and those over a certain age"—he winked at Chris—"let us say forty, ordinarily plan to stop in the mountain town of Orisson for the first night rather than attempt the Pyrenees in one day. Though only eight or so kilometers to Orrison—not quite five miles—it is all uphill, and still leaves seventeen kilometers for the rest of the hike over the Pyrenees the next day."

"That sounds like a good plan," Emilee said. "Should we make reservations in Orrison? Can we?"

"Reservations?" Chris said. "We're pilgrims. Where's your faith?"

"O ye of little faith, eh?" Gino, the Italian, said. His clerk was on the phone again, standing in the doorway to the back office.

"We of little stamina," Emilee said.

The French clerk frowned at Chris and Emilee's *credenciales*. "Someone has been using my ink. That will not do for your first stamp. Let me get a fresh pad and new *credenciales*—won't take a minute. We must start you off right." He exited for the back office.

"Is this your first time?" Chris asked Gino.

"This is my first Camino, my first pilgrimage, but I have trekked across much of Europe."

"This is our first time. We're in-between jobs—well, we got canned—and thought we would come walk the Camino and seek some guidance. We're determined to hear from God."

Gino looked very interested. "Truly?"

Chris and Emilee's clerk returned and addressed Emilee as he unfolded the new *credenciales*. Chris continued to speak with Gino.

"I have not seen Melanie smile in a long time," the clerk said.

"Oh, you know the hotel owner?" Emilee said.

Chris glanced over momentarily at the mention of Melanie, but continued his conversation with Gino.

"*Oui,*" the clerk said, "But I have not seen her smile lately."

"We were kind of surprised by it ourselves this morning," Emilee said.

"Poor woman, her husband is dying of some kind of cancer. She spends the nights in the hospital with him."

"Oh, that's sad. What does *le Notre Père* mean? She kept mentioning it."

"*Le Notre Père* is the Our Father—'Our Father who art in heaven.' The Lord's Prayer, *oui?*" He stamped the new *credenciales*. "That's better. Here you are."

"Ready?" Chris said. He and Emilee stood.

"Be sure to get the hiking pole, my friend," Gino said.

The next man in line stepped forward to take Chris' seat, and as he did he held up his hiking pole for Chris to see. "A good stick," he said, "used properly, can take twenty-five percent of the pressure off your joints, they say."

"Buen Camino," the clerk said to them.

"Buen Camino," said another man in line.

"Buen Camino," said two or three other people in line.

CHAPTER 8

Crossing the Pyrenees

The red tile roofs of Saint Jean receding behind them, Chris and Emilee, amid a string of pilgrims, ascended the narrow paved road leading into the Pyrenees. Like the others, they wore backpacks, hats, and hiking boots—and carried their newly purchased walking sticks. Like the others, their faces beamed with anticipation.

"We're really doing this," Chris said between breaths. "Five hundred miles. This is awesome."

Emilee smiled at him.

The clerk had been right about the steepness of this first leg of the journey, and before long Chris and Emilee were breathing heavily, and the string of pilgrims had spread out, with greater gaps between them.

"And you're awesome, too," Chris said. "How many wives would do this with their husbands?"

Emilee gathered her breath. "Perhaps one less if she had known she'd be panting within an hour. *Le Notre Père*"—she paused for another deep breath.

"What?" Chris said.

"*Le Notre Père*—that French phrase Melanie kept repeating in the jeep—the guy in the office said it means the Lord's Prayer. She was telling us her husband was praying it while listening to the music."

Chris thought about that. "Hmm…." he said.

The Pyrenees Mountains form an imposing natural border between France on the north and Spain on the south, stretching 270 miles from the Mediterranean Sea to the Atlantic Ocean. The Roncesvalles Pass, which Chris and Emilee were attempting, was one of the few in the range accessible by foot, a fact that had made it the locus of a number of important historical events, including the two famous Battles of Roncesvalles, the first in 778 when Charlemagne's rear guard was ambushed in the pass by the Basque—the event out of which grew the legend celebrated in *The Song of Roland*—and the second in 1813 when Napoleon's forces prevailed over the English and Portuguese in a battle of the Peninsular War.

Two routes led over the pass, both beginning in Saint Jean. The Valcarlos route, which followed the highway through the valley, was the easier one, being a bit shorter and not nearly as steep. Nevertheless, the Napoleon Route, which Chris and Emilee were walking, was more popular with pilgrims, due to its quiet mountain paths, spectacular views, and, yes, its difficulty—pilgrims who made the twenty-five kilometer hike (about fifteen miles), cresting the high point at Col Lepoeder at nearly a mile above sea level (4,688 feet; 1,429 meters), felt a tremendous sense of accomplishment as they descended to the little Spanish village of Roncesvalles below. It was a bracing start to the Camino.

Chris and Emilee were laboring seriously less than five kilometers out of Saint Jean. Their breaths were ragged, sweat rolled down their necks and backs. Chris glanced over his shoulder. The line of pilgrims was thin now.

"Whoa. Let's catch our breath," he said.

They slipped off their packs and sat on rocks in the grass beside the road, and took long drinks from their water bottles. Shaggy sheep with distinctive black faces—the Laxta breed, developed by the Basque—grazed on the deep green slope below. A cowbell rang from one of the farms scattered through the foothills. And Emilee noticed a wide variety of birdsong—tweets, trills, chirps, and a squawk or two—without any competition from car engines, AC units, lawnmowers, radios, power tools.

"My backpack is hanging a little heavy to my left," Chris said.

"Mine to the right," Emilee said.

They took a few moments rearranging the packs' contents, centering the weight. They were Osprey "Anti-Gravity" backpacks, Chris' a burnt orange and Emilee's a powder teal. They were anti-gravity in name only.

A twenty-something hiker trotted up the road, his shirt off, his backpack strapped to a well-muscled and tan frame. Chris and Emilee gawked as he ran past them.

"I'm right behind you," Chris called after him.

The runner waved over his shoulder.

"I'd take my shirt off too," Chris said to Emilee, "but I don't want to get a sunburn."

Emilee laughed.

"What?" Chris said. "Would you be embarrassed if I took my shirt off?"

"*I* wouldn't be embarrassed," Emilee said.

More hikers made their way up the road and past them. Gino, the handsome Italian from the Pilgrim Friends Office, was one of them.

"*Bene*, you bought poles," Gino said.

"They're already helping," Chris said.

"Buen Camino," Gino said.

"Buen Camino," Chris and Emilee said.

They resumed walking after a few minutes and shortly afterward turned left onto a dirt path at a sign which read: "Refuge D'Orisson - 2 km."

"Just a little more than a mile," Chris said. "I don't know about you, but I definitely want to stop in Orisson for the day."

"Definitely," Emilee said.

They were following a paved road again as they rounded a green slope and suddenly saw the Refuge D'Orisson up ahead. They breathed sighs of relief. It was a picturesque building, a rectangular, two-story cabin with a stonework facade. It backed up against the mountainside and looked out over the road upon the breathtaking valley below.

"Our first *albergue*," Chris said, consulting his guidebook. "Twenty-eight beds." He pulled out his *credencial.* "Get out your pilgrim passport to show we deserve a bed."

They both noticed Gino in the outdoor café across the road from the *albergue*. He sat at a small table with a pretty young woman, smiling charmingly at her and leaning in, as though taking her into a confidence.

Chris and Emilee wiggled out of their packs as they entered the door of the albergue. A kind-eyed clerk with a neatly trimmed gray goatee smiled at them from behind a counter. They placed their *credenciales* before him.

"You don't know how glad we are to see you," Chris said. "We thought about walking all the way to Roncesvalles, but reality set in. We'll stay the night."

"I'm sorry, *monsieur*, but all the beds are taken."

"Tonight?" Chris said.

The clerk nodded.

"By pilgrims?" Chris said.

The clerk nodded.

"But it's not even noon," Chris said.

"Did no one tell you?" the clerk said. "Because of the difficulty of this first stage of the Camino, crossing the Pyrenees, the Refuge D'Orisson is a rare case—a pilgrim hostel that encourages reservations. So you can break the first stage into two days. Did no one tell you?"

Emilee looked at Chris.

Outside, they continued walking up the inclining road, the chatter from the pilgrims at the outdoor café across from the Refuge D'Orisson fading behind them.

"Well, it saves us some euros," Chris said.

"I don't know if I have another seventeen kilometers in me today. What is that, ten miles?" Emilee said.

"But we'll start down the mountain sometime." He nodded at a group of hikers ahead of them on the road. "They didn't stop at the albergue."

"They look half our age."

Several kilometers later they seemed to have emerged at the top of the world, the road leading through treeless green fields and unobstructed views in all directions. Griffon vultures, with swooping wing spans of nine feet, soared above, effortless on warm updrafts. In the valleys below, clouds clung like cobwebs to rounded green hills.

Up ahead they saw other pilgrims veering off the road toward a cluster of white rocks on a gentle peak, where a statue of some sort stood. Chris consulted his guidebook and learned it was La Vierge d'Orisson, an image of the Virgin and Child. They crossed the grassy field with the others and picked their way through the rocks to the Madonna, draped with rosaries and flowers. The Madonna, along with the Babe in her arms, seemed to cast a watchful gaze over the valleys below.

An hour or two later, Chris and Emilee, their faces dangerously red, followed a dirt path that skirted a stand of tall mountain trees. They passed an upright stone slab which read: "Saint-Jacques de Compostelle - 765 kms." They glanced wordlessly at it.

A little later the path suddenly came upon a very welcome sight, a large slate-gray water fountain in the middle of nowhere, fronted by a stone patio. There was a large name on the fountain: "FONTAINE DE ROLAND." A line of pilgrims stood in front of it, awaiting their turn at the water.

Chris and Emilee walked up to the end of the line, mouths hanging open, breathing heavily. They took out their empty water bottles.

They stood behind a blond teenage boy, who, when he heard their breathing, turned and looked at them. The boy then whispered in the ear of the blond man in front of him—obviously his father—who turned and looked at Chris and Emilee, smiled, and said in a German accent, "*Bitte*, take our place. Sir, madam, please." Then he and the boy stepped aside so Chris and Emilee could take their place in line.

Chris shook his head. "Oh, no, no."

The man said, "Please, we insist." Then he and his son stepped behind Chris and Emilee.

"Well, okay," Emilee said. "Thank you so much."

The next three people in line—red-haired young women wearing Trinity College Dublin windbreakers—also turned and insisted that Chris and Emilee move forward. Chris laughed and Emilee hugged them. And so it continued, one pilgrim after another stepping out of the way, until Chris and Emilee were standing at the fountain.

"Do we look that bad?" Chris said.

"We are all fellow pilgrims," said someone from the line.

"Plenty for everyone," someone else said.

"'Even a cup of cold water in my name,' *ja*?" the German father added.

Chris nodded and filled their bottles.

After a short rest, they waved goodbye to those who remained at the "FONTAINE DE ROLAND" and continued on the path with smiles, the stone patio receding behind them.

Chris looked at his guidebook. "That was also the border," he said. "We're in Spain the rest of the way."

Emilee looked up at clouds rolling in.

Before long, the footpath led through a forest again. Chris and Emilee were the only pilgrims in sight. A few fat raindrops fell.

"We better put our jackets on," Emilee said.

They slipped off their packs and—*CRACK!*—

lightning struck somewhere nearby on the mountain. They practically jumped out of their boots. Suddenly, rain poured, drenching them. Giving up on their jackets, they grabbed their packs and sticks and ran for the cover of the trees—until another *CRACK!*—a bolt above the trees—stopped them.

"*Pellegrini!*" a voice called. "This way."

They turned to see Gino running past them, pointing ahead. They saw, through the blurring rain, the small stone shack he was pointing to, and ran after him. He reached the shack and ducked in the open door. They followed him through the door, rivulets of rain dripping from their hats, faces, and backpacks.

"The *Americano* and *la bella donna!* Bad luck, eh?" Gino had to yell to be heard above the pounding rain. He was not as soaked as they were, wearing a poncho over both his clothes and backpack.

"Should have bought umbrellas too!" Chris said.

Emilee dug towels out of their packs.

"May I suggest ponchos, my friends?" Gino said. "They are light and cover all."

Gino looked around. "What is this place?" He took a flashlight out of his pack and shined it around the interior of the shack, revealing one window in a side wall, an old ash-black fireplace in the back wall, a discarded table and bench, a half-erected pup tent, chopped wood, and, scrawled all over the walls in a dozen languages, messages left by pilgrims over the years. "Many have come before us," he said. "Perhaps seeking shelter too."

Later they sat on the bench and looked out the open door. The rain had stopped, and leaves dripped pleasantly outside the shack.

"No, I have not heard of Grand Rapids. New York, Chicago, Las Vegas, these I have heard of."

"You're from Italy?" Chris said.

"To be more precise, from Sicily."

"Shhh!" Emilee said. "Look."

Two horses, a dam and her foal, approached a puddle on the mountain floor and drank gracefully. The dam and foal were light brown with cotton-white feet and manes.

"Wild horses, a mother and her offspring," Emile whispered. "How beautiful. I wish Riley and Quinner were here."

She took out her phone and snapped a picture. The animals finished drinking and walked away without a care in the world.

"I'll be right back," Chris said.

He exited the hut and, as Emilee and Gino watched, went about gathering stones. He returned with two handfuls, placed them at their feet, and retook his seat.

"What are you doing?" Emilee said.

"Remember Rambo the Priest said pilgrims write their burdens on stones and carry them to the Cruz de Ferro, the Iron Cross, later on the pilgrimage? We need to do ours."

"So many?" Emilee asked.

"One for each burden," Chris said.

"Couldn't you have remembered *after* we got over the mountain?" she said.

"May I have one?" Gino asked.

"Yes. Please." Emilee said.

Chris dug a black Sharpie out of his pack. "See, I planned for some things." He took a stone, prepared to write, but paused with a self-conscious glance at Gino.

Gino stood, palming his stone. "I must ponder my words. The clouds are clearing. Buen Camino." He exited.

Chris and Emilee again seemed to walk on top of the world, bare mountain heights stretching in all directions. It was late afternoon. The route led gradually upward, step after step, and they struggled more than ever, faces hot and sweaty, breath husky— which the altitude did not help.

Heads drooping, they walked on, leaning heavily on their walking sticks, until finally Chris put a hand out and touched Emilee's arm, and they stopped. Without bothering to leave the trail, Emilee let her backpack slip off her shoulders, dropped her stick, and put her hands on her knees. Chris forced her water bottle into her hand and, without straightening, she sloshed water on her face and then the back of her neck.

Chris drank long and hard from his bottle and looked toward a peak to the south, the highest peak visible—a round green mound of a mountain.

Chris cracked a smile. "You know what this is, Em?"

Still bent over, she shook her head.

"A mountaintop experience."

"I will hurt you," she said.

"Seriously"—Chris consulted his guidebook—"that's Collado de Lepoeder, or however you say it. About 4,700 feet tall, the high point of the day. It's downhill the rest of the way. See."

Emilee straightened up and looked ahead and some relief came to her face.

The descent was deceptive. As they wound down a rugged mountain path in the last of the twilight, they here and there, through a break in the trees, caught glimpses of Roncesvalles below—a forest-fringed village of twenty buildings nestled around a monastery—and it seemed they must reach their destination soon. But the trail kept going on and on, long past darkness—complete darkness, but for an occasional tantalizing flash from the village below.

At a bend in the path, Chris' boots slipped out from under him—from loose dirt or gravel—and he slid into the dark gray trunk of some otherwise invisible tree.

"Ouuuuuuch!" he said.

"Are you all right?" Emilee said.

Chris groaned quietly. "Scraped my knee."

"This is dangerous," Emilee said.

Chris stepped back onto the trail and they continued walking. "Let's add flashlight to the list of supplies we need to buy," he said.

"And a first aid kit."

Finally, they made it down the mountain. They emerged from the trees and walked slowly up the wide gravel road toward the albergue, a big, white, three-story block building with shutter-framed windows. Their faces were gray with fatigue, Chris' pants were torn over the left knee, and Emilee labored heavily under her pack. They passed clotheslines strung with shirts and hiking pants and thick socks, and wooden benches and picnic tables in front of the building—but no sight of pilgrims. They reached the brick pavement in front of the entrance, walked by a sign reading, "Albergue de Roncesvalles," and entered the door under the archway.

The albergue host regarded them quizzically as they approached the lobby counter and placed their *credenciales* before him.

"You are arriving only now?" the host said. "We have no rooms."

Chris and Emilee stared opened-mouthed at him.

"I am afraid you have lost what the pilgrims call the bed race, *mis amigos*. It is still the busy season. All the beds are taken."

"But the guidebook says there are 183 beds," Chris said.

"*Sí*, and all are taken. I am afraid you have missed the meal as well."

"But you don't understand," Chris said. "We didn't start in Orrison today, but walked all the way over the Pyrenees, twenty-five kilometers."

"The Camino de Santiago gets more popular each year. Our beds have been taken for hours and most of the pilgrims are already asleep to get an early start tomorrow."

Emilee's eyes welled. "What do we do?"

"Some pilgrims camp when necessary."

"We're not prepared to camp," she said.

"You can try the private hotels, but they are quite busy too, and without a reservation.... And of course they are more expensive."

"I don't care how much they cost," Emilee said.

The host picked up a brochure off the counter and handed it to Chris. "Here's a list. They are within walking distance."

Emilee sat at one of the picnic tables outside the albergue, resting her head on her folded arms. Out of the corner of her eye she noticed the albergue host step out of the door for a moment and look at her. She heard Chris' footsteps returning from the village, and looked up—but he shook his head.

"I would have paid any price, but all the rooms are booked, most for months by some tour group," he said.

She noticed that he limped on his right foot as he

circled the table to sit heavily beside her. They sat quietly a moment, then he lay his head down on his folded arms.

"You're limping," she said. "Your knee?"

"A blister on my foot. I started feeling it on the way down."

"*Señor y señora.*" They turned to see the albergue host approach. He carried a red nylon tent bag, a Ziploc bag with sandwiches, and bottles of water. "Here is a tent left behind last year. You may have it." He handed the bag to Chris and placed the sandwiches and water on the table, then he walked back toward the albergue door.

"Oh, thank you so much," Emilee said.

"Excuse me," Chris said.

The host stopped and turned.

"Could we borrow a flashlight so I can see to set this thing up?"

The host nodded, and Chris stood and followed him to the door.

They set up the tent between two dark beech trees about thirty feet off the Roncesvalles road. Emilee held the flashlight as Chris pounded the last tent peg in the ground.

"Doesn't look great, but it will—" Chris started to say, but the light went out as Emilee crawled in the tent.

Chris crawled in beside her, picked up the

flashlight, switched it on. It was a one-man tent and a tight fit. Emilee lay on her back, still in her jacket, eyes closed, feet poked between the packs at the other end. Chris looked at her face.

"Goodnight?" he said.

No response.

"Tomorrow has to be better," he said.

Emilee answered without opening her eyes. "You said to leave the planning for this pilgrimage—what little there would be—up to you. Didn't you read anything about this bed race?"

"I saw it mentioned on a blog but just skimmed over it—I didn't plan to do any racing. I didn't know it was a literal race."

Emilee let out a long, frustrated breath—through her nose, because her lips were pursed tightly.

"Maybe it won't be so bad. Maybe—"

"We'll talk about it tomorrow," she said.

Chris opened his mouth to respond, but, still watching her face, thought better of it.

He set the flashlight at his side and leaned forward to remove his right boot, revealing a bloody sock at the heel. He pulled the sock down and in the flashlight beam inspected a punctured, oozing blister. The skin had peeled partially away. Cringing, he pulled it the rest of the way off and threw it out the tent flap. He pulled the dirty sock back up, flipped off the flashlight, and lay back with a tired sigh.

A moment passed in the dark.

"Goodnight," Emilee said.

"Goodnight, babe," Chris said.

CHAPTER 9

Surprises

The next day, as the morning sun streamed through the beech branches, Chris stuffed the tent bag in his backpack. He and Emilee slipped their backpacks on and set out, not down the road with the other pilgrims, but back toward the albergue. Their faces were puffy, their clothes wrinkled, and their steps stiff. Emilee put a hand on the small of her back.

"I don't know if I hurt more from the hike or the ground," she said.

Chris grunted.

"We need warmer jackets," Emilee said.

Chris nodded.

Ten minutes later they sat on a bench outside the albergue entrance, their shoulders slumped, their packs and sticks beside them. Chris' right boot was off.

"You'd think they'd at least let us shower and change," Emilee said.

Chris shrugged. "Even hotels have check-in times."

Gino walked up. "The *Americano* and *la bella donna*." He looked them over, noting Chris' torn pants and bloody sock. "A rough walk down the mountain? Remember, I am counting on you to show me that faith pays."

Chris noticed that Gino didn't look a hundred

percent himself. His eyes were bloodshot, he squinted as though suffering a headache, and his smile didn't reach his eyes.

"But why are you here, and not walking?" Gino asked.

"We got in late and had to sleep in a tent. We're going to hang around here today, get a bed tonight, and get up early tomorrow and get on the winning side of the bed race. Why aren't you walking?"

"I, too, am going to stay at the albergue tonight. I am, uh, not feeling well."

"Oh, I'm sorry," Emilee said.

Gino walked away and entered the albergue.

"I wonder what's wrong with him," Emilee said.

"I saw him flashing his pearly whites at a woman in the hotel bar last night, nothing but a bottle of wine between them. Remind me not to leave you alone with him."

Emilee gave Chris a surprised and offended look, but, thinking it over, decided he deserved a fond smile instead.

They checked in as soon as the dayshift host permitted, showered, napped, and by the time other pilgrims began arriving for the night, they were sufficiently rejuvenated—stiffness and soreness aside—to offer hopeful "Buen Camino"'s to them.

That night they sat in the albergue dining room with the other pilgrims, eating voraciously and chatting amiably at long white tables with matching benches. No other furnishings were visible in the well-lit, tidy hall, giving it a monastic feel. There was not an empty space on any bench. Chris and Emilee sat in the middle of one of the tables, talking to the guests on either side of them, Chris to an older South African gentleman (who was biking the Camino) who had pulled up an old book on his phone to show Chris. "It is the *Codex Calixtinus*," he said in his country's particular variant of English accent, "written by a monk who walked the pilgrimage in the twelfth century. It's the oldest guidebook about the Camino, in fact the oldest guidebook period. You can download it free online."

"Cool," Chris said.

As he looked up from the South African's phone, Chris noticed Gino two tables away, smiling at the red-head beside him and doing more talking than eating.

In addition to being one of the largest albergues on the Camino, the Roncesvalles Albergue was also one of the more up-to-date, having been freshly renovated in 2011. Semi-enclosed compartments lined the dormitory walls, each with two sets of bunks. As lights went out, some pilgrims chatted quietly or plugged in their phones or walked with a toothbrush to the rest room, but Chris, one arm sprawled over the side of the upper bunk, was already fast asleep, and Emilee, lying on the bunk below him, lay with her eyes closed and her face relaxing—

"You know it's true!" snapped a female voice.

Emilee's eyes popped open with a start. The words had come from a pretty young woman sitting cross-legged opposite a young man on the other lower bunk in the compartment. Her eyes, big and brown, flashed angrily at him.

"I thought we could both use some getting in shape," he said, "but that's not why—"

"Shh, Nick!" the young woman said, noticing Emilee's open eyes. "Did we wake you?"

"Sorry," the young man said.

He had a Spanish accent and the woman a slight French accent, but different from those Emilee had heard in Saint Jean. They were so cute—the young woman with her thick, chocolate waves, and the young man with his close-cut black curls—that Emilee couldn't be angry.

"It's not your fault. I'm a light sleeper," she said.

"Not your husband—he is a corpse," the young man said.

"I'm tired, Nick," the young woman said.

Nick stood. He was short, compactly built, and wearing nothing but boxer shorts. Emilee colored and averted her eyes as he climbed to the top bunk.

"Are all albergues mixed-gender?" Emilee asked.

The young woman shrugged.

"I believe so, but not all so nice," Nick said.

Emilee closed her eyes. "Another little surprise."

CHAPTER 10

Bienvenidos!

Early the next morning, in the predawn dusk, Chris and Emilee exited the albergue and, with others, set off on stage two of the Camino Francés, Roncesvalles to Zubiri. It was another long stage (twenty-two kilometers, or almost fourteen miles), but according to the guidebook would be flat or even mildly descending most of the way. They wore their backpacks and carried their walking sticks. Chris limped noticeably and Emilee yawned.

The route followed highway N-135 for a short spell, passed the famous "SANTIAGO DE COMPOSTELA – 790 km" sign, the first road sign for the Camino inside Spain.

"Just 490 miles to go," cracked one pilgrim.

Soon the route left the road for the forested trails and farmland paths it would follow most of the day. They passed through a number of small towns, none with a population exceeding 500. They passed through Burguete, which had been mentioned in Hemingway's *The Sun Also Rises* and still boasted a piano (in the Hotel Burguete) with the storied author's signature on it. They passed through Espinal, which had been founded in the thirteenth century as a haven for pilgrims from bandits, and through Linzoain, a hamlet of white stone walls and brown roofs, with a church that also dated from the thirteenth century (the ancient dates never ceased to amaze the New World-ers Chris and Emilee). As they walked by the church, an old-timer, sitting on a bench, raised his pipe to them.

Later in the day they stopped at a food truck parked on the shoulder of a winding rural highway. Emilee stood in line at the food truck window, rubbing her shins, while Chris sat with their backpacks on a patch of grass in front of the truck, his right boot and sock off as he showed his blister to a Korean family, who shook their heads in sympathy.

At the Alto de Erro, the descent to Zubiri began. The trail down was rather steep, rocky, and at points slippery, and after the long day of hiking, eighteen kilometers behind them with five more to go, they would have taken it very slowly—if not for the bed race. So, with little talk and much support from their hiking poles, they worked their way down without a rest—or a fall.

They entered the albergue lobby, tiredly and nervously eyeing the host as he checked in the couple ahead of them. The couple left and Chris and Emilee stepped forward and placed their *credenciales* on the counter.

"Two beds, please," Chris said.

"Certainly, *señor*. Sixteen euros," the host said.

Chris and Emilee shared a relieved smile. Chris paid the host with euro notes. The host returned Chris' change, took his ink pad, and stamped their *credenciales.* "*Bienvenidos!*" he said.

About one hour after the lights had been turned out that night in the Zubiri albergue dormitory—men and women asleep on bunks up and down the room, two or three snoring—a ringtone sounded, playing the *Star Wars* theme. Several people in the vicinity stirred, including Emilee, who lifted her head from the pillow. Chris, in the bunk above, slept on. The ringing continued; awakened pilgrims grumbled. Finally a man got out of his lower bunk, crossed the aisle, and shook the shoulder of a man on a top bunk, who opened his eyes in confusion.

"Your phone is ringing."

"Oh! Sorry."

He fumbled with his pillow, located the phone, and turned it off. The other man shook his head and returned to his bunk. Emilee sighed and was about to lay her head down when she noticed Gino several bunks away, leaning on his elbow and dealing cards to himself. He nodded and smiled at her. She lay her head down.

CHAPTER 11

The Scallop Shell

Chris and Emilee walked with Gino under a bright sun the next day, following a paved road that descended through green hills toward Pamplona. The route had followed the Arga River much of the day, crossed medieval bridges, cut through old towns, skirted modern highways, passed fertile fields.

"Yes, from Sicily," Gino answered Chris. "The birthplace of...." He looked at the pavement and didn't finish his statement.

"Pizza?" Chris said.

"Chris," Emilee said.

"Ah, *Americani*," Gino said.

A side path leading from a farmhouse joined the road a short distance ahead. Two pilgrims—the German father and son from Roland's Fountain—exited this path and joined the Camino trail a few feet ahead of Chris, Emilee, and Gino.

"Buen Camino," the man and son said.

"Buen Camino," Chris, Emilee, and Gino said.

Chris noticed the scallop shells tied to the Germans' packs. He asked Gino, "What's the meaning of the shells I see everywhere—on people's packs, road signs, shop windows?"

Gino shrugged.

Chris looked at the shell tied to Gino's belt. "You're

wearing one."

"When in Rome, no?"

The German father looked over his shoulder. "They are scallop shells, *meine freunde*, symbols of Saint James the Apostle. One interpretation is that the lines on the shell represent the various paths of the Camino that all lead to one destination, Santiago. Others say the lines represent the fingers of an open hand, the generosity that should characterize pilgrims and those who would aid them."

"I like that," Emilee said.

"Pamplona ahead, the most populous city on the Camino Francés, and which your Herr Hemingway made famous for the Running of the Bulls—but we are too late for that." The man and his son walked on ahead.

"Would you run with the bulls, Chris?" Gino asked.

"Maybe."

Emilee laughed.

"I might," Chris said, defensively.

Gino smiled. "Not with that limp, my friend."

Pamplona is a city of some 200,000 people. Pilgrims had to maneuver busy city streets before passing through the gate of Old Town Pamplona, which was alive with cafés, shops, pilgrims, and tourists. Though the day remained bright, Chris, Emilee, and Gino strolled in the shadows of colorful four- and five-story buildings, which consisted of lofts built above small shops. The buildings lay side by side, without an inch of space between them, on both sides of gray brick streets too narrow for sidewalks.

"How do one million people fit in this city for the Running of the Bulls?" Chris said.

They stopped in front of the Caminoteca, one of Old Town's pilgrim outfitters. Chris and Emilee slipped out of their packs and placed them beside other packs in the street (proprietors did not like pilgrims bringing their bags inside with them). They started inside, but Gino stood where he was.

"Aren't you coming?" Chris asked.

"I'll watch the backpacks. I, uh—I don't need anything."

Gino watched through the window as Chris and Emilee walked between the aisles laden with hiking supplies—backpacks, hydration systems, tents, guidebooks, hats, boots…. Despite his words, he watched with envy on his face. He turned away and surveyed the street, his eye falling on a trio of pretty tourists, a bar at the corner farther down, and a cream-colored tower of the cathedral.

There was, oddly enough, a Burger King in Old Town Pamplona, where Gino wanted to stop. They sat at a window table, Emilee tying scallop shells to their backpacks while Chris transferred items to the jackets they had just purchased. Gino, munching on *Patatas Clásicas* (French fries) and drinking a Coke, watched

Chris transfer a compact Bible to the right front pocket of his new coat.

"Those are nice new jackets," Gino said.

"We needed something warmer," Emilee said.

"They're Patagonia Puffs," Chris said. His jacket was electron blue and Emilee's French red. "Not cheap, but the clerk says they're water-repellent, warm, and pack down small. You look like you could use something warmer."

Chris decided against transferring his wallet to the new coat, and instead stuffed it in his backpack and zipped it up.

At the heart of Old Town Pamplona is the Plaza Consistorial, or Town Hall Square, where the Fiesta de San Fermín (which includes the Running of the Bulls) begins and ends each July. Chris, Emilee, and Gino stopped when they reached the gray-bricked square and looked up at the ornate, five-story, flag-bedecked building on the other side.

"That's City Hall, according to the guidebook," Chris said, "and this is the square where the Camino route intersects the bull's route."

Emilee smiled with amusement.

"I might do it," Chris said.

"I believe I will stay and sightsee in this old town. I hope we meet again down the trail," Gino said, patting Chris on the shoulder and nodding at Emilee. "Buen Camino."

"Buen Camino," Chris said.

Emilee watched him walk away. She said to Chris, "Well, we're staying in this town too."

"I think Gino's idea of sightseeing might be different than ours."

Chris and Emilee stayed in an albergue on the outskirts of Old Town (there were many albergues to choose from in Pamplona). The dormitory lights still on, pilgrims chatted, folded laundry, listened to their earbuds, tapped tablets. Emilee, her robe pulled tight around her, walked between the rows of metal, squeaking bunks (all together in one open room) and turned down the restrooms hall, only to find a trash can blocking the women's door. Instead, women were lined up outside the men's room door on the other side of the hall. The albergue hostess emerged from the women's room, holding a wet plunger and shaking her head. She exited the hall.

"The toilets are backed up," a woman in the line explained to Emilee. "We have to use the men's room."

Frowning, Emilee got in line.

A man walked up behind her. "What's up here?" he asked.

"Our toilets are backed up," another woman in the line said. "We have to share."

The man shrugged and stood behind Emilee. Emilee waited a moment, stepped out of line, and returned to the dormitory where Chris lay on his bunk reading John Grisham's *The Testament*.

"The women's toilets are stopped up. We have to use the men's," Emilee said.

"Bummer. Okay," Chris said.

"No, it's not okay. I want you to come and stand behind me in line to make sure no other man enters while I'm in there."

"Oh. Sure."

Chris climbed down. Taking an exasperated breath, Emilee turned and retraced her steps through the dormitory.

CHAPTER 12

Nick and Louise

They awoke while it was still dark the next morning, and the days that followed, to hit the trail by daybreak. It was a grueling schedule. Up with the dawn, twenty-four kilometers from Pamplona to Puente la Reina. Up with the dawn, twenty-two kilometers from Puente la Reina to Estella. Up with the dawn, twenty-two kilometers from Estella to Los Arcos....

But it kept them on the winning side of the bed race.

The hikes were harder on Chris, not only because of his blister, which never got enough rest to heal, but because he had come to the Camino completely out of shape. The nights in the albergues were harder on Emilee—late night chatterers, bathroom traffic, snorers. In one albergue, she had to shiver through a cold shower—the hot water ran out just as she stepped under the showerhead—and in another albergue there was an unfortunate incident with another hiker. They had returned to the dormitory after a change-of-pace dinner in town to find a man about their age lying on Emilee's bunk. "Oh," Emilee said with surprise. "That was my bunk. I left my hat and walking stick on it. Didn't I?"

The man shrugged and pointed to a nearby upper bunk. "You mean those?" he said. "This bunk was empty. Besides, I have bad knees—or I'd give this bed up for you, is what I mean."

"Come on, man," Chris said. "This is my bunk up top. Of course, she had this one."

"I'd give it up," the man said, "but my knees."

Emilee took a frustrated breath. "Never mind," she said and crossed the aisle to the other bunk.

"Buen Camino," Chris said angrily to the man.

"You too," the man replied.

The countryside continued to charm—picturesque medieval towns, windmills on rolling hills, seas of golden wheat. The climate became more Mediterranean as they left the Pamplona basin and entered wine-growing country. They followed country roads that led through red earth vineyards and olive groves. In green meadows shepherds tended their flocks with the help of watchful dogs. Old bridges spanned rivers and streams.

Every day seemed a history lesson. Before they had left the suburbs of Pamplona, they had passed the plains where Charlemagne's 100,000 soldiers had defeated a Muslim king's equal force in a bloody battle. They walked through towns that had barely survived the Black Death in the fourteenth century, a church founded in the twelfth century by the Knights Templar, and roads and bridges laid down by conquering Romans. Town after town boasted some ancient church, castle, or hermitage (or their ruins). Dates from the thirteenth or fourteenth century ceased to impress, or at least surprise, after the monastery in Irache dating from 958 and the battlefield in Los Arcos from 914.

Modern Spain consists of seventeen "autonomous communities," regional authorities similar to Canadian provinces, that have been cobbled together from the various local kingdoms that spread throughout Spain over the centuries. The Camino Francés passes through four of them: Navarra with the capital of Pamplona; La Rioja, the winemaking region; Castilla y León, the nation's largest region, where about one half of the Camino is walked; and Galicia, where the Camino's destination, the city of Santiago de Compostela, lies.

Chris and Emilee entered Castilla y León about midday on the eleventh day of their journey and stopped at Redecilla—population 137, according to the guidebook. They sat outside a little stone-walled restaurant at a bright red table proudly sporting the Coca-Cola logo (with matching chairs). Chris had removed his right boot and placed it on the table beside a balled-up napkin and an empty *Matutano Fritos* bag. He rested his right foot, still in its sock, on his knee as Emilee read out loud from her phone: "'Blisters are small pockets of fluid that collect under damaged skin'—Yada, yada—'It's important to avoid bursting the blister— '"

"There was no helping that," Chris said.

Emilee continued reading: "'If it does burst, don't

peel off the dead skin.'" Emilee looked up at Chris.

"It was just hanging there," he said.

"'Cover the area with a dry, sterile dressing to protect it from infection,'" Emilee read.

Chris pulled down the sock, but only so he could see, not Emilee. The Band-Aid, stained with blood and pus, didn't quite cover the open sore, and the surrounding skin was angry red.

"This one isn't cutting it," he said. "Let's stop at a drug store."

"'If new hot spots form, take a break, dip feet in a cool stream—'" Emilee broke off reading as the young couple at the next table began to raise their voices in anger.

"And Daphne and Chloe!" the young woman snapped. "Why did I let you take me away from them for six weeks?"

"We've already called them a thousand times!" the man said. "Anyway, they're used to staying with your mother. Don't worry, they don't miss us."

"Oh! How can you say that?" the woman said.

"But I thought—"

"We wouldn't have left them if they were yours!" the woman said.

The young man slapped the table and spoke for a moment in rapid-fire Spanish. Chris and Emilee couldn't help but turn and look.

"You know I love them more than anyone in all the world," the young man said.

The young woman noticed Chris and Emilee looking their way. "See, you are disturbing them," she said.

Emilee recognized them as the cute couple from the Roncesvalles Albergue, the young woman with the big brown flashing eyes and thick dark tresses and the compactly built young man with close-cut black curls.

"Oh hi," Emilee said.

The young couple took a moment to recognize her, then smiled politely, if stiffly.

"You know each other?" Chris said.

"We woke her up fighting. Like we're doing now," the woman said.

The man shook his head apologetically. "No, no," he said.

"You may as well be honest. We have been fighting this whole trip."

An uncomfortable silence followed. After a moment Chris stood and extended his hand to the young man. "I'm Chris. This is my wife, Emilee."

"I'm Nick, and this is my—"

"I am Louise," the woman said.

"You have a lovely accent," Emilee said. "Are you French?"

"I am French-Canadian, from Montreal," Louise said. She nodded coldly at Nick. "He is from Cuba."

Another uncomfortable silence....

"How did you meet?" Emilee asked.

"I worked on a cruise ship with a port of call in

Miami," Louise said, "where he had come to live."

"I sold T-shirts and souvenirs to tourists. We have been married a year now," Nick said.

"And already he is tired of me."

"Louise!" Nick protested, then looked at Chris and Emilee with upturned hands. "It is not so."

"Well," Chris said awkwardly, "we had better get back on the trail."

Louise stood. "I will walk with you, Emilee."

"Sure," Emilee said slowly, with a glance at Chris.

She and Louise slipped on their backpacks and started walking.

Nick looked up at Chris.

"Come on," Chris said.

They walked for some time with little conversation, accompanied by the buzz of traffic from busy highway N-120, which the Camino had paralleled much today. Louise and Emilee walked ten feet ahead of Nick and Chris, who was limping more than ever.

Emilee looked at Louise, who walked with her eyes straight ahead and her lips pressed tight. "It's a pretty countryside," Emilee ventured.

Louise didn't answer.

Emilee gave Chris a glance and shrug over her shoulder.

"So Christian radio hosts?" Nick said to Chris. "You mean, DJs?"

"Were. Might be again. We got fired. We came on

the Camino to get away from it all, spend some time with each other, and hopefully find God's will for us."

"Have you found it?"

"I don't think we've even had a chance to look yet, we've been pretty beat up."

Louise had been listening to their conversation. "Why don't you tell them why we came on the Camino, Nick?" she said without turning around. "Why you brought me?"

Nick let out a frustrated breath, shaking his head.

"It's because I've gained weight since we got married," Louise said.

Emilee turned and frowned at Nick.

"It's ridiculous, Emilee," he said. "That's not why."

"I have not gained weight?"

Nick looked helplessly at Chris.

"But you're adorable," Emilee said.

"Yes, but you should have seen me when I was a cocktail waitress on the cruise ship, before I quit my job for him." She stopped and turned to Nick. "Give me your phone."

They all stopped and Nick handed over his phone. Louise thumbed through some pictures on it, found what she was looking for, and showed the picture to Emilee and Chris. Chris' eyes widened.

"You see? That is my cocktail skirt."

Emilee frowned at Chris and pushed the phone back to Louise. They continued walking.

"So he brings me to Spain to walk off my extra

weight. And he wonders why I do not want to make love—because I do not feel pretty."

Emilee's eyes widened and she looked down at the trail, face turning red. Chris rubbed his forehead, hiding his eyes.

Nick spoke in rapid, exasperated Spanish. Then he turned to Chris. "Does it make sense that I want to make love all the time—she says—but she also says I don't think she looks pretty?"

"Then why did we come to do this, if not for me to lose weight?" She looked at Emilee. "He admitted the other night it was to get me in shape."

"I said we were both getting back in shape."

"Then why did we come?"

"Because I thought God might help us, in our marriage."

"I know you will leave me someday for a prettier girl. Well, maybe I will leave first."

"Okay now," Emilee said. She put an arm around Louise's shoulder. She turned to look at Nick. "Why don't you and Chris walk ahead of us for a while. Some distance. We'll be along."

Nick nodded in quick agreement and he and Chris passed the women.

CHAPTER 13

One

They slept that night in Belorado, a town of about 2,000 dating from the Roman era. Lights long out in the albergue, Chris slept deeply on a top bunk, Emilee on the bunk below his. The beds were arranged lengthwise in this albergue, head to foot, head to foot, from one end of the dormitory to the other. The man in the lower bunk nearest Emilee's head, sleeping with his head toward hers, snored heavily and regularly. Suddenly he expelled a loud honk, startling Emilee, whose eyes peeked open as she frowned.

The man's regular snores continued, and she turned on her side—until another honk from him. She raised her head to look at him, and his regular snores continued. She sat up, picked up her pillow, placed it on the opposite end of the bed, and lay down on it.

A woman slept in the lower bunk on this end of the bed, her head now toward Emilee's. As Emilee's face began to relax, the woman mumbled, giggled, and mumbled some more in her sleep: "... down the mountain ... my hair. It doesn't work ... text me the cookies ... Buen Saint James ..."

Emilee groaned quietly. "Are you kidding me?" she said. She rolled on her stomach and pulled the pillow over her head.

The next morning, with the dormitory panes still dark, Chris stood beside Emilee's bunk, took the pillow off her head, and nudged her shoulder. She groaned, rolled on her side, and opened her eyes sleepily.

"Do we have to leave so early today?" she said.

"If we want a bed tonight."

They reached Villafranca, a town on the doorstep of the thickly wooded Oca Mountains, after a twelve kilometer walk, and made sure to stop at the Supermercado (which, in spite of its name, was no bigger than a 7-Eleven), for the guidebook said this was the last chance for another twelve kilometers to stock up on water and provisions. After visiting the store, they sat on a guardrail of the highway—national road N-120—which cuts noisily and, for hikers, dangerously through Villafranca on its way to the mountain pass.

Emilee removed insoles from a package and inserted them in her boots. "This is supposed to help with shin splints," she said. "And if we could avoid hard surfaces… " She watched Chris unwind a four-inch strip of duct tape. "Men and duct tape. How's that supposed to help?"

"It creates an additional rubbing surface over the blister."

"You need such a wide strip?" She leaned toward Chris. "Let me see that blister."

Chris drew his foot back to keep her from seeing. "This will help it get better." He applied the duct tape over the bandages on his heel.

"Maybe we should rest a few days," Emilee said. She offered a flirtatious smile. "We could have a second honeymoon."

Chris paused for a moment as he slipped on his boot. "Very tempting."

"Get a hotel, with a private bathroom, hot showers, soft sheets, no one snoring but you, no rush—"

"You mistake me for a man with a job and a paycheck. We really can't even afford these albergues." Chris stood. "Ready?"

Emilee sighed and stood. "You're no Gino. Or Nick."

They followed earthen paths up into the pines and quickly realized today was going to be one of the more difficult hikes. Not only because it was a long stage, twenty-eight kilometers from Belorado to Agés (leaving sixteen still to go), but because it led up and over steep hills. The Oca Mountains had been known in medieval times as a haven for bandits; even today, but for the hiking path, the woods seem remote and wild. They entered Agés about sundown, passing a hand-painted road sign that declared: Santiago 518 km.

"We're one third of the way there," Chris said.

The next day the trail led to Burgos, one of the bigger cities on the Camino with a population of

180,000. The approach was an unpleasant walk along the A-1 highway and past factories, but the city itself was delightful, filled with historic architecture and magnificent art (including, in one fifteenth century monastery, a golden *retablo* crafted from gold Christopher Columbus brought back from the new world). Chris and Emilee presented their *credenciales* at the Casa de Cubos, the city's largest albergue with 150 beds.

At dusk they sat eating in the crowded dining room when Nick appeared in the door, anxious eyes searching the tables, until he located Chris and Emilee.

He came quickly toward them. "She's going to leave me," he said.

His desperate look and tone made all the guests stop eating and talking and look at him.

"I got us a room in a hotel," he continued, "to give her a break and Skype our girls and sightsee for a couple days, but she thinks I did it to—well, you know what she thinks! She tells me to find a marriage counselor—tonight, in a foreign country!—or she's leaving. I walked out, said maybe I won't come back, but—" He ran his fingers through his tight curls. "You are old and married."

"Thanks?" Chris said.

"Will you come and talk to us?"

Emilee looked at Chris. They stood and followed Nick away from the table, Chris grabbing a roll to take with him.

It was a plain but comfortable hotel room, with a queen size bed, on the edge of which Nick sat; two upholstered arm chairs, in which Chris and Emilee sat; and a writing desk with a vinyl rolling chair, in which Louise sat with her legs crossed fiercely.

"Well, you know, men and women are wired differently, have different needs," Chris said.

Louise jumped to her feet, pointing at Nick. "He has one need!"

Nick shook his head, mumbling angrily in Spanish.

"What? Say it in English," Louise demanded.

"I wish you had only one need. If I could be so lucky!" Nick stood. "I buy you this, I buy you that—" He turned to Chris. "It's never enough."

"I quit my job for you!" Louise said.

And so it went, and worse, for the next hour or so. Louise would stand at the foot of the bed with arms crossed, speaking hotly, as she looked back and forth between Nick at the head of the bed and Chris and Emilee in the chairs. Then Nick would pace back and forth, speaking rapidly and with much hand motion, as Louise sat shaking her head, a smirk on her pretty lips. Eventually they stood yelling at each other, as Chris and Emilee looked on with pale faces—and a knock came on the door. The manager warned them that he would call the *policía* and have them removed from the hotel if the fighting continued. Nick nodded apologetically and gave his assurances, and the manager, after a warning frown at everyone in the room, departed.

Nick closed the door and he and Louise stood at opposite ends of the bed, not looking at each other, breathing heavily.

Chris looked at Emilee.

"The first years of a marriage are often the most difficult," Emilee said mechanically, just to say something.

Louise crossed her arms. Nick shoved his hands deep in his trouser pockets.

"Excuse me for a minute," Louise said, and walked into the bathroom and closed the door.

Nick said some words to himself in Spanish, then grabbed the plastic ice bucket off the desk and exited the room.

Chris whispered to Emilee, "We need to get out of here."

Emilee nodded. "This is a disaster. I don't think we've said one thing to help them."

"Let's just read some Scripture—do something spiritual— and leave."

He took his compact Bible out of his jacket pocket as Louise and Nick reentered the room and sat tiredly on opposite ends of the bed.

Emilee said, "I'm sorry we haven't been able to help you, but—"

Chris broke in: "Let me read you what Jesus said about marriage—it's real short—and then we have to go." He turned to the Gospel of Matthew, chapter 19, and began to read, not looking up. Emilee kept her eyes on the page as well.

> *Some Pharisees came to him to test him. They asked, "Is it lawful for a man to divorce his wife for any and every reason?"*
>
> *"Haven't you read," he replied, "that at the beginning the Creator 'made them male and female,' and said, 'For this reason a man will leave his father and mother and be united to his wife, and the two will become one flesh'? So they are no longer two, but one flesh. Therefore what God has joined together, let no one separate."*
>
> *"Why then," they asked, "did Moses command that a man give his wife a certificate of divorce and send her away?"*
>
> *Jesus replied, "Moses permitted you to divorce your wives because your hearts were hard. But it was not this way from the beginning."*

After Chris finished reading, he and Emilee kept their eyes down for a few moments. When they looked up, they were surprised to see both Louise and Nick crying and looking softly at each other.

"I am sorry, Nicky," Louise said.

"I will never walk away, Louise."

They took each other's hands.

"We are one?" Nick said.

"Always, Nicky."

They continued to look in each other's eyes, and eagerly.

"Maybe we should go," Emilee said.

Neither Louise nor Nick protested. In fact, Nick gave a little nod, without taking his eyes off Louise. Smiling, Chris and Emilee stood and exited.

CHAPTER 14

Hospital

Leaving Burgos, the Camino enters the Meseta, the geographical region that covers most of Spain. Dry, barren plains stretch from horizon to horizon. Medieval pilgrims often complained of losing their way in the featureless landscape of the Meseta, endless wheat fields upon endless wheat fields. Some modern pilgrims skip the region altogether, to save time or to save their bodies—and perhaps souls—the wilderness experience (in the summer, the sun blazes; with the change of season, chilly winds sweep across the plains). Chris was determined to walk it, limp and all.

The first day on the Meseta is one of the longest walks of the Camino, more than thirty-one kilometers (almost twenty miles) from Burgos to Hontanas. Along the way they stopped in the little town of San Bol—so small it had but one albergue with twelve beds—to soak their feet in a local fountain, which according to legend had healing powers. Chris' limp persisted as they returned to the trail.

The walk through history continued in the Meseta. One day they passed under the hilltop ruins of a castle built by Julius Caesar before the birth of Christ. On another day they stopped in a town (Carrión de los Condes) that had observed the same Thursday market day since 1618 and boasted a monastery turned albergue that had housed Saint Francis on his pilgrimage.

They began to notice buildings of a different type as they passed through the villages—churches, albergues, and homes built of adobe or mudbrick, for stone was hard to come by in the Meseta. There were also charming dovecotes and odd *bodegas,* wine cellars built into hillsides, like hobbit homes.

They passed the halfway point to Santiago a few days into the Meseta, but by then the long desolate roads and monotonous landscapes had so sapped their energy and enthusiasm that it was a "glass-half-empty" moment. They barely remarked on it, and Chris walked a little slower.

After a week on the Meseta, it was a relief to draw near León, which the guidebook described as a "vibrant metropolitan area of some 200,000 souls." But the approach to the city was bereft of pilgrim glamour, following busy highways through industrial parks and mundane suburbs.

Chris and Emilee walked on an asphalt lane separated from the highway by a mere white line, cars and trucks roaring by. A galvanized crash rail, bordered by trees, enclosed the other side of the lane. Scallop shells and yellow arrows painted on the blacktop were the only reminders of pilgrimage.

Chris leaned heavily on his walking stick whenever his right boot came down. He kept falling a little farther behind Emilee, who walked with her eyes down, her thoughts turning. After a while, she realized Chris wasn't beside her and turned to see him limping along about twenty feet behind her.

She waited for him. "Can you keep going on that?" She nodded at his heel. "Really, maybe we need to rest."

"I was just daydreaming," Chris said as he caught up to her and hobbled by.

But not ten minutes later, as they approached a corner, Emilee again realized that Chris had fallen back and turned to see that he had come to a complete stop on the path, about forty feet behind her. He leaned on top of his staff, face etched with pain. As Emilee strode toward him, he took a seat on the asphalt.

"Let me see that blister," Emilee demanded.

Chris removed his boot, his sock, the duct tape, the bandage—and Emilee caught her breath at the sight. A large patch of outer skin on Chris' heel had rubbed away entirely, all the way to the pale white under-skin oozing blood and pus. The surrounding tissue, tinged with sickly yellow hues, peeled and flaked away. A hot red aura, tinged with dark streaks, radiated from the wound.

"Yeah, I don't think I can keep going," Chris said.

"Keep going? You could lose your foot! That's infected."

"It's just a blister."

Six or seven pilgrims approached on the lane,

young men and women.

"Will you help me with my husband? He can't walk anymore. I need to get him to a doctor."

"Emilee, don't be ridiculous."

She put a hand on his shoulder and prevented him from standing. He didn't fight her.

"What's the problem?" one of the men said.

But no answer was necessary when they saw his heel; their mouths dropped open. They helped Chris up. One took his backpack, another his stick, and two others got up under his arms to support him.

"Luckily, we're entering León," another pilgrim said. "We'll find a clinic here."

Emilee's eyes welled. "Thank you."

"I don't need to see a doctor," Chris said.

"Maybe you need a psychiatrist," a third pilgrim said. "What are you doing walking on that?"

"It's just a blister," Chris said.

The first pilgrim arched his eyebrows and said, "American?"

"Yes," Chris nodded.

The pilgrims nodded to each other.

The clinic was a standalone building with a sign over the glass entryway that read: "Centro de Salud." The same two pilgrims who had gotten under Chris' arms on the path helped him through the sliding doors, a third following with his pack and staff—the others had stayed on the trail, watching over their three friends' packs. The sliding doors remained open as they deposited Chris and his pack and staff in front of the check-in desk, waved goodbye, and got hugs from Emilee.

Chris sat on an upholstered exam table, sterile paper crinkling under his heel, which rested on the slide-out leg extension, and which the doctor studied closely.

The doctor nodded to Emilee. "It is indeed infected, *señora*." Then he said to Chris, "You could not see that for yourself?"

"I thought I'd just walk and pray through it."

"You are a pilgrim on a medieval trail," the doctor said, "which I hope to walk myself someday, but you are under no obligation to follow medieval medical practices. This wound is in danger of sepsis, which puts not only your foot in danger, but your life. I am checking you into a hospital room and ordering an antibiotic drip."

The doctor walked away. Chris stared after him.

It was dark outside the hospital room window. Chris lay despondently on the covers, his arm attached to an IV bag hanging on a portable pole by the bed. He looked glassy-eyed at his heavily bandaged right foot. His left foot wore a non-slip hospital sock. Emilee sat in a chair by the bed contemplating his face with concern.

"You should get a hotel room," Chris said.

"We can't afford one. Besides, I wouldn't want one without you."

Chris responded dispiritedly, "You should get one."

Emilee, reclining awkwardly on the hospital sleeper chair, awoke to the day nurse changing Chris' bandage.

"Perhaps a little better, *Señor* Danielson," the nurse said. Then to Emilee: "We were trying not to wake you."

"Did I hear 'a little better'?" Emilee asked.

The nurse nodded.

Emilee gave Chris a hopeful smile. He managed a morose shrug.

The nurse gathered her tray of tools, checked the IV bag, and walked out the door.

It was dark and windy outside the hospital room window, trees somewhere below scraping against the building. Emilee tossed and turned on the too-short sleeper. Chris slept with his bandaged foot outside the covers.

The day nurse—her name was Teresa—and Emilee stood looking at Chris's heel, the nurse holding fresh bandages. The old bandage, stained light pink with blood, lay discarded at the foot of the bed.

The nurse gave Emilee an encouraging smile. "*Está bien*," she said. "Better."

Emilee nodded politely but still frowned.

"Better," the nurse said as she lifted Chris' heel.

Two days later the curtains were thrown open on a sunny afternoon, and Chris stood looking out the window, his weight resting on his left foot, his bandaged right foot balanced on the toe. He had wheeled the IV rack to the window with him.

Emilee wasn't present.

The doctor entered the room and stopped when he saw Chris at the window, looking toward his heel. "Ah, *peregrino*," the doctor said.

Chris turned, awkwardly.

The doctor smiled. "You are protecting that heel?"

"Yep."

The doctor motioned toward the bed. "Let me see."

It was night again outside the room window, as the orderly wheeled the IV rack out of the room. Emilee stood out of the way and watched with relief. Chris reclined on the bed, studying his right heel, now minimally bandaged.

The next day Chris sat with a pillow behind his back against the raised bed, both his feet in no-slip socks now, though a small bandage peeked out of the right one. Emilee stood looking out the window, and Chris watched her uneasily.

"I don't want to quit," he said.

Emilee walked over and sat by the bed. "Who said

we would?"

"Really?" Chris said.

"Remember when we were just starting, heading into the mountains, and you asked, 'How many wives would do this with their husbands?'?"

"Yeah," Chris said. "You're awesome."

"How many husbands want God's will so much they'd be willing to walk 500 miles to find it? *You're* awesome."

"Or crazy?"

"Another possibility. Chris, we've been so overwhelmed we haven't cracked his Book, and we came here to hear from him."

Chris nodded at his coat lying on his backpack. Emilee went to the coat, took out his Bible, and returned to her chair. For the next half-hour or hour—they lost track of time—they took turns reading aloud a verse that came to mind, pausing to think about it, then sharing their thoughts with each other. A seminar they had attended called it "Bible Meditation for Couples."

At one point Chris found Hebrews 11:8 and read: "*By faith Abraham, when called to go to a place he would later receive as his inheritance, obeyed and went, even though he did not know where he was going.*" He stared at the page for a moment, then looked up and said, "I like to think we came here by faith. On this pilgrimage."

"I see no other reason why we're here."

"What if it was just my own foolish presumption?" Chris said as he handed the Bible to her.

"Then it would be *our* foolish presumption." She turned toward the middle of the Bible, found Proverbs 3:6, and read: "*Trust in the Lord with all your heart and lean not on your own understanding.*" She looked up from the page, pondering what she had read. Then she said, "Trust in him even when life doesn't seem to make sense."

Chris felt a wave of peace wash over him at her interpretation, and he let out a slow breath and nodded.

She returned the Bible and Chris read the next verse in Proverbs: "*in all your ways submit to him, and he will make your paths straight.*" He looked up slowly, thoughtfully. "Keep him in mind—honor him—and he'll get you where you need to be."

They nodded at each other, and exchanged an encouraged look.

CHAPTER 15

News from Home

Chris, his spirits lifted by Emilee's love and the Bible's promises, felt better until it was time to check out of the hospital. Then he and Emilee sat across from the accounts administrator, a smartly dressed woman named Benicia, Chris scowling at the bill and tapping his credit card on the desk. The cubicle around them was composed of light blue fabric panels.

"We'll have to make payments," Chris said.

"Well, I don't know—" Benicia began.

"That'll have to do, unless you'll take an arm and a leg," Chris said.

Benicia gave him a quizzical look.

"He's trying to make a joke," Emilee said.

"A pint of blood? A pound of flesh?" Chris said.

"Do you not have health insurance in America?" Benicia said.

"Funny," Chris said. "But it will cover very little of this. We had to scale back to bare bones coverage when we lost our jobs."

Chris offered the card. Benicia attempted to take it, but Chris did not let go. "You can put $225 on that, not a penny more."

Benicia frowned, took the card, began to process it.

"I thought you had socialized medicine in Spain and Europe?" Chris said.

"*Subsidized* medicine, *Señor* Danielson—there are always costs. And you are not a citizen of Spain or the EU with the appropriate cards. Are you?"

"I'm feeling the love here," Chris said.

Emilee shook her head at him.

When they exited the hospital, through the lobby doors, Chris was still scowling. They stopped on the sidewalk to slip on their packs.

Emilee's phone rang. She looked at the screen. "It's Tyler." She put the phone to her ear. "Hi, Pastor. It's nice to hear from you. I hope everything's okay?"

Chris whispered to Emilee, "I asked him to check on our house."

"Yes, he's right here, Pastor. Tell Rebecca hi."

She handed the phone to Chris.

"Hi, Tyler. How's it going?"

"We miss you guys," Pastor Tyler said. "How's the walk across Spain? About finished?"

"Still a couple hundred miles to go. It looks like it's going to take a little longer than we thought."

"Learning a lot?"

"About blisters."

"Huh?"

"Long story. How's the house?"

"I went by again yesterday."

"I really appreciate that, Pastor."

"Checked inside, out back. Everything looks okay."

"Great."

"Did you loan your car out?"

"What do you mean?"

"It wasn't in the garage. I think it was there last time—wasn't it?"

"That's where we left it. I didn't loan it out. What do you— It wasn't there?"

"No."

"Are you sure?"

There was quiet on the other end of the line.

"Pastor?"

"I don't think I could have missed it."

Now it was Chris' turn to be silent.

"Chris, it sounds like it could have been stolen."

Chris closed his eyes and ran a hand through his hair.

"Chris?" Pastor Tyler said.

"What's wrong?" Emilee said.

Chris sat on the curb.

An hour later they were still outside the hospital, sitting on a bench near the lobby, Chris on the phone with their next door neighbor.

"Yeah, Trent, my pastor called and the police will be sending a unit by. They'll probably want to talk to you, the nearest neighbors. Did you see anything? Anything missing?" Chris listened. "Well, that's good for you. I also called Ray." Chris listened. "Yeah, it's a bummer. Thanks."

Chris disconnected and handed the phone back to Emilee. He noticed tears in her eyes.

"Riley's and Quinner's car seats were in it," she said.

She dug for a tissue in her backpack.

"Emilee," Chris said.

She kept digging.

"Emilee," he repeated, and waited for her to find the tissue and look at him. "I never sent in the car insurance payment, for the renewal. I had it ready to go, but after we lost our jobs I didn't have the stomach to part with the money."

"Oh, Chris."

CHAPTER 16

Storia Famigliare

Chris and Emilee didn't talk much on the route out of León. They both felt as if they had just been run over, and their encouraging time of Bible meditation already seemed a long time ago. Chris felt about two inches tall for having failed to renew the car insurance, and they both worried about their rapidly dwindling finances and lack of a job.

It didn't help when the route passed the luxurious Hostal San Marcos, where many pilgrims stopped to take pictures, because this is the hotel in the movie *The Way* where Martin Sheen's character put up his fellow pilgrims for the night. The hotel is one of Spain's *paradores,* government-restored historical structures, often castles or monasteries, refurbished to preserve an Old World feel. The now-exquisite Hostal San Marcos had once been a fifteenth-century pilgrim hospital. Chris and Emilee just kept walking.

"Maybe I need to call pastor about the Family Ministry position," Chris said as they crossed an old stone bridge over the Rio Bernesga. "And withdraw cash to last us the rest of the trip—stop using the cards and we might spend less."

"The *Americano* and *la belle donna!*"

They turned to see Gino walking up behind them with a bright, carefree smile.

"I would have thought you well down the Camino by now?" Gino said.

"You too. What are you doing here?" Chris said.

"I've had a run of luck—God has smiled on me—at the casino here in León."

Chris looked at Gino's new jacket, a pullover puff with a brick pattern like Chris', but chromatic yellow.

Gino noticed Chris' look. "It's a Patagonia, like yours. No more cold walks."

"New boots too," Chris said.

Gino nodded. "But what about you?" he said. "Why aren't you farther along the way?"

"I've been in the hospital with an infected blister."

"You're luck has not been so good," Gino said.

"That's not the half of it."

"Let's walk together. You can tell me about it."

They continued together across the bridge.

The route continued several kilometers through the suburbs of León and then followed highway N-120 westward, meaning that the exit from the city had as little pilgrim vibe as its entrance.

"… and to make matters worse I forgot to renew the insurance," Chris said, glancing over his shoulder at Emilee, who had fallen about forty feet behind the men to let them talk.

"You have had bad luck indeed," Gino said. "Have you found the guidance you came to seek?"

Chris put his hand on the jacket pocket that held his

Bible, but answered Gino with a shake of his head.

Gino continued: "You are walking to hear from God and I am walking to—" Gino looked away for a moment. "But I am smiled upon and you are suffering. How do you explain this?"

Chris shook his head again.

Very late in the afternoon, they reached the town of Virgen del Camino (about 5,000 residents), where they decided to stop for the night. It was only eight kilometers outside of León, but they had gotten such a late start on the day.

They entered the municipal albergue, a large one with forty beds, and approached the tall man behind the counter, who spoke first: "*Bienvenida, peregrinos.* Three beds?"

"I was afraid we might be too late."

"The bed race has come and gone this year, I think," the host said. "It slows down just enough with the cooler weather."

"No more bed race!" Emilee said.

"So the blister was a blessing in disguise?" Gino said.

"It wasn't on your foot," Chris said.

Chris, Emilee, and Gino walked together again the next day, a pleasant route that spent much of the day alternating between a quiet rural road and an earthen track. Chris and Gino found themselves walking ahead of Emilee again. Gino took a stone out of his coat pocket, the stone he got from Chris at the mountain hut, and thumbed it absently. Chris saw the Italian word *Storia* written on it.

"*Storia*?" Chris said.

Gino looked at the stone in his hand, just noticing it. "Yes. *Storia*—it means history."

"History is your burden?"

"There was not enough room for *storia famigliare*—family history," Gino said. "I mentioned my home is Sicily. It's an island famous for many things—the largest by size in the Mediterranean. Our fortified Marsala wines. An active volcano, Mount Etna. And one more thing—" Gino looked at the stone in his hand. "You've heard of *la mafia*? It too had its birth in Sicily, growing out of the private armies wealthy landowners hired to protect their estates in lawless times, but became—well, you know. It has lost much of its influence, but some refuse to let it die."

They walked quietly for a moment, Gino still looking at the stone, Chris staring at Gino.

"Your family is part of the Mafia?" Chris said.

"No, no, no. My father was a hanger-on, who fancied himself a retainer, but I am afraid he was nothing more than a petty criminal, who spent most of my childhood in prison, and died there."

"I'm sorry."

"But my older brother has aspirations, as do his friends. And when he learned a certain vintner played a part in our father's final imprisonment, he—" Gino paused and gave Chris a sidelong look. "You are a Protestant priest of some kind, no?"

"I'm ordained, if that's what you mean," Chris said.

"So you cannot divulge my confession."

"I'm not sure that would hold up in—" Chris began.

Gino waved his hand dismissively. "I can speak confidentially with you. When he learned the vintner violated the *omertà*—the code of silence—he said it fell to us to avenge our father. So to prove my allegiance, he gave me the honor of executing the vengeance." Gino let out a breath, looked at the stone in his hand. "So I am here."

"You killed him?" Chris said, aghast.

"No, no. I do not have the courage for that, or the darkness of soul—*grazie a Dio*. I robbed him and disappeared. But I doubt it satisfied my brother."

"Wow," Chris said.

The route had become a paved road again as they reached the outskirts of Villar de Mazarife, where, on a brown brick patio enclosed by a decorative metal fence, a pilgrim mosaic stood. Several hikers had stopped to view the mosaic and chat.

"So you see why I must walk the Camino, the sins I must pay for, my own and my family's."

Emilee called to Chris: "Honey, the Casa de Jesús Albergue is the least expensive." She was consulting the guidebook. "Take the next left, on Calle Corujo. It's a little early, but the doctor said you shouldn't overdo it."

Gino extended his hand. "I will keep walking. No more casinos ahead, but private players have a way of sniffing each other out. So while my luck is good...."

CHAPTER 17

The Cruz de Ferro

After his conversations with Gino, Chris felt worse than ever. He could not help but compare Gino's good fortunes with his own bad—the good luck of a casual believer with the beat-downs of a serious one. For this reason, he was all the more eager to reach the Cruz de Ferro—the Iron Cross, which the priest in the Grand Rapids travel agency had told him about—to lay down his burden stones. The logical side of his mind, the theologically trained side, told him there was nothing magical about a wayside cross on a medieval pilgrimage, that he could release his burdens to God any time through prayer. But the truth was, he had felt drawn to the Cruz de Ferro ever since he first heard of it—for some reason. And now it was but two stages away.

Pastor Tyler called with the police report as Chris and Emilee followed the quiet country road out of Villar de Mazarife. Chris practically ground his teeth as he listened to the police's summary of the crime. Who were these people to come and take their vehicle? What had Chris and Emilee done to them? Why hadn't God prevented it? He found himself thinking fondly of God's Old Testament acts of vengeance.

"Thanks for the update, Pastor," he said. "We know

you have other things to do."

He disconnected and said to Emilee, "Police say they got in through the side door from the yard, that rusty lock. Say we were lucky they didn't get in the house." He frowned bitterly. "I hope the ignition coils fail again."

About halfway through the day, they came to a famous thirteenth-century bridge with twenty arches and a cobblestone surface, which led into the town of Hospital de Órbigo. As they tread the cobblestones, Emilee read from the guidebook. "This is the Paso Honroso Bridge—or 'Honorable Pass Bridge'—and it was the site of a legendary jousting competition in 1434. One brave knight taking on all comers because his heart had been broken by the woman he loved. The Spanish are very romantic."

Chris cracked a smile. "I've always wondered if I might have some Spanish blood."

"Well, sweetie, you can set your mind at ease," Emilee said.

By the next day, they had left the Meseta and were climbing into the Cantabrian Mountains, an ascent that would take them to the very high point of the Camino Francés—higher than the crossing of the Pyrenees. Their legs and lungs burned in earnest after Santa Catalina, and the guidebook told Emilee it was still some sixteen kilometers to the day's supposed destination, Foncebadón.

"It's uphill all the way to the Cruz de Ferro," she said. "Which, lucky us, happens to be pretty much the highest point on the Camino."

They walked past a six-foot-long arrow, composed of stones, which lay in the middle of the path and pointed ahead.

"But I suppose it's fitting the cross is the highest point," she said.

Chris nodded.

A few hours later, they were still climbing. It was overcast and windy, their faces as red from cold as from the climb, their jackets zipped to the collar. They breathed heavily, especially Emilee, who walked with her head drooping. Chris looked at her, then at the approaching village.

"How far to the cross?"

Emilee raised the guidebook, then said between breaths, "The village up ahead... is Rabanal... Then seven more kilometers after that... All uphill."

"Tackle it tomorrow?" Chris said.

Emilee nodded.

The seven kilometers up the mountain to the Cruz de Ferro the next morning followed a rocky, puddled trail, and the light rain turned to ice pellets that blew in their faces as they neared the summit. The trail, as it approached the Cruz de Ferro, fell in line with a paved road on which slow-moving tourist vehicles traveled, as well as bicycling pilgrims. The trail and the road led through a forest of mountain trees.

"Woohoo!" a bicyclist called and pointed. "There it is!"

Chris and Emilee quickened their pace, the trees gave way, and they saw the Cruz de Ferro standing alone in a clearing up ahead. The iron cross itself sat atop a tall wooden pole that jutted out of a giant mound of gathered stones—stones that have been piling up for centuries. Pilgrims congregated all about the site, several standing on top of the mound around the pole. Bicyclists and tourists took pictures from the road. Others milled in front of a modern stonework chapel across a grassy field.

Chris and Emilee, their pace slowing as they surveyed the site, approached the base of the mound, stepping through loose stones scattered about. They stopped and looked up at the cross. Then they slipped off their backpacks and took out their burden stones. Emilee took out a single stone, which she looked at, and which read: "Our future." Chris took out five stones and cupped them in his hands.

They waited for the pilgrims at the top to descend and then they climbed the mound carefully. When they reached the wooden pole, they looked at the wide variety of mementos tied or tacked to it: photos, a military medal, postcards with scribbled prayers, a fabric star, a rosary, a child's stick-figure drawing, scallop shells, a rusted key, a broken watch, and a single hiking boot. Around the base of the pole were other items, including a deflated American football, painted stones, a canteen, and more hiking boots and shells.

Emilee placed her stone at the foot of the pole, closed her eyes, and prayed. "Please take care of that for us, Lord. I believe—I know..." Tears escaped her eyes. "I know you will. But it's hard to see right now." She opened her eyes, wiped her tears, and looked at Chris.

He frowned at the stones in his hands, which read: "Fired," "Closed doors," "$" "Ministry," "???"

Emilee put a hand on his shoulder.

He closed his eyes and prayed. "Lord, we've served you our whole life. I thought. But we have nothing to show for it. Just a boot in the pants everywhere we turn. We're broke and getting broker. We came on this pilgrimage—I dragged my wife here, halfway around the world—"

"No," Emilee said quietly.

"—to get direction and maybe some comfort, but it seems like we've been run over by a truck instead. And all I have to show for it is a hospital bill I can't pay." He opened his eyes and glanced skyward with an embarrassed half-smile and shrug. "Sorry for all the complaining. But those are my burdens." He laid the stones down.

CHAPTER 18

Awkward

As they walked away from the mound of stones, Chris glanced back at the cross, then smiled at Emilee. "I feel better after that prayer," he said.

"Me too."

Chris patted his backpack over his shoulder. "Of course, dumping those rocks doesn't hurt."

The route continued downhill, along a curving paved road, until the Refugio de Manjarín came into view—a rustic stone and wood albergue and shop bedecked with bright flags and banners. In front of the shop, a stack of hand-painted wooden signs pointed to cities in all directions and gave their distances, including: "Santiago 222 km," "Roma 2475 km," and "Jerusalem 5000 km." Bikes and backpacks awaited their owners outside the shop, and a few pilgrims sat at a picnic table behind a low stone wall.

Emilee looked at the guidebook. "This sounds like an interesting place. It's donation only, so it's in our price bracket. Offers a communal meal. Run by a certain Tomás, who claims to be the last of the Knights Templar, the ancient protectors of pilgrims, and—" She stopped reading and shook her head. "But no electricity or running water, and the bathroom is an outhouse."

Chris stopped. "Gino!"

Gino sat at the picnic table across from two twenty-something females. He turned and looked. "Chris. Emilee," he said without enthusiasm.

Chris and Emilee approached the table. The two females stood and walked away, rather quickly. Chris asked, "Did you stop at the cross?"

Gino, whose face was lined with fatigue, crossed his arms and rubbed his shoulders for warmth; he was not wearing his new coat. "Last night, briefly. Then I came here for a bed." Gino paused, and looked from Chris to Emilee—but at mid-jacket level, not in their eyes—without a smile. "You?"

"Just coming from there. We're headed on now, if you...." Chris was going to ask if Gino wanted to join them, but his words trailed off at the lack of response from Gino. "Well, I guess we'll get going. Buen Camino."

"Buen Camino, my friends," Gino said.

Chris and Emilee walked away, continuing down the paved road.

"That was awkward," Emilee said.

"Yep," Chris said.

CHAPTER 19

Unheard of!

The next morning Chris sat on the edge of Emilee's bunk, already dressed, except for his right boot and sock. He leaned over, examining and touching his heel where the blister used to be. He began to pull on his sock as Emilee woke up.

"Morning," he said.

"How long have you been up?" Emilee asked. She looked around the small dormitory; all other beds were empty.

"My heel feels a little hot. We walked farther yesterday. I guess because it was downhill after the cross. I think we should take a break today just to be safe."

"Okay."

"I'm going to go soak it in the stream." He stood. "You can stay in bed, the host said there's no hurry. I gathered our dirty clothes in my pack—their washing machine is still down—and I'll wash them in the stream."

"Stay in bed, let my husband do the laundry. No argument from me."

Chris, wearing his jacket and carrying his pack, entered the woods across the road from the albergue, and sidestepped his way between thick oaks, tall leafy bushes, and heavy scrub to the clear-flowing stream.

He selected a spot near a chest-high boulder protruding from the brush, removed the drawstring laundry bag from his backpack, and began to dip the articles one at a time in the cold water. He slowly worked his way farther and farther from his backpack, which he left leaning against the boulder, as he laid out the wet garments one after another on a series of rocks along the bank.

Then he removed his right boot and sock, sat on the bank, and sank his foot in the water with a shiver (the water was fresh off its mountain course).

He took his Bible out of his jacket pocket and revisited some of the verses he and Emilee had read together in the hospital. He had drawn such peace and encouragement from those moments, and wanted to remind himself of the promises they had read.

He heard footsteps on the forest floor, and the rustling of bushes, and looked over his shoulder; the sound came from somewhere in the woods behind his backpack and the boulder. "Emilee?" he called. "I'm over here."

The footsteps stopped.

"Over here," Chris repeated. He closed his Bible and put it in his right jacket pocket. He called over his shoulder again. "This water's freezing. Why did you get up?"

No response.

He pulled his dripping foot out of the water, reached for a towel, and stood, looking in confusion toward the woods. "What are you—" he began, but never finished, because at that moment a man's hand reached around the boulder, took the backpack by the shoulder strap, and yanked it out of sight—and boot steps beat away through shaking foliage.

"Hey!" Chris cried, and, his right foot bare, ran awkwardly after his backpack, first along the bank, then sliding around the boulder, then ducking into the brush. "Hey! I need that!"

Branches slapping across his face, Chris weaved through the trees, following flashes of his orange backpack through the scrub ahead. He lost sight of it, but kept crashing through the branches and around bushes, his eyes searching the greenery. Suddenly, circling a tree, he came upon the backpack, lying in the soil at the foot of a bush. He stopped and went to it, but kept peering through the woods for the thief.

"I can't believe this," he muttered.

He bent to pick up the pack.

A fearful cry, like that of a cornered animal, sounded from behind a tree and, before Chris could turn, a blow cracked down on his head—right above the corner of his right eye—a brief, painful explosion. He moaned and slumped to the ground, hearing the back of his jacket tear on a rock as his world faded to black.

Twenty minutes later, a hand on his forehead above his eye, Chris walked dizzily through the woods.

"Chris? Where are you?" Emilee called from somewhere, and it slowly dawned on Chris that she had been calling him for some time now.

He saw his backpack under a tree and aimed for it.

"Chris?" Emilee called again, and there was more worry than irritation in her voice now.

"Over here."

Chris reached the backpack, went down on one knee, and looked inside the main compartment, which was still open.

Emilee stepped out of the bushes. "There you are. What are you doing? Why don't you answer me?" She walked toward him, but stopped and gasped when she saw the blood and the big purple bump over his eye.

She rushed to him. "What happened?"

"Someone followed me in here—I guess—and tried to steal my backpack. I chased him and got hit—I think with a walking stick. I feel like I'm going to throw up."

She bent to look at the swelling, almost touched it, but pulled her fingers back.

Chris ruffled through the backpack. "Stole my wallet. Our cash. My bank card. Credit card." He patted his chest and arms. "And my jacket."

"But are you all right?" She pulled a tissue from her pocket and began to clean up the blood. "Why did you chase him?"

Chris sat on a bench outside the albergue as a female EMT put the finishing touches on the bandage

126

on his forehead—attaching the thick square of gauze with medical tape. Gathered around were Emilee, the albergue host, and curious pilgrims. The ambulance, the side panel of which read Emergències Mèdiques, was parked in the road, a male EMT lounging by its open back doors and smoking a cigarette.

"*Señor*," the female EMT scolded, "concussion symptoms can mimic those of more serious injuries, such as a cerebral contusion—that is, a bruise of brain tissue—or a hemorrhage. That is why procedure calls for immediate evaluation."

"I'm not doing another stint in the hospital."

"You lost consciousness and—"

"Not doing it."

The EMT stepped back to examine her work. She sighed, then turned to Emilee. "Is he always so stubborn, *señora*?"

"Chris, you said you felt like you were going to throw up, and you were dazed," Emilee said. "We should make sure you don't have a more serious injury."

Chris glanced at the ambulance and shook his head, which made him wince.

"*Señora*, at the least, no more walking until he is asymptomatic—all symptoms gone."

Emilee nodded.

The next day, freshly bandaged—the EMT had been kind enough to leave gauze and tape—Chris sat in the albergue dining hall with the host, Rubén, and a uniformed police officer. The officer spoke in Spanish and Rubén translated.

"Of course, they will look for a man in a blue hiking jacket, Officer Ortega says, but the thief, unless he is a fool, will not walk around in it but hide and sell it. Probably for the same reason he left your pack—too conspicuous."

The officer spoke in Spanish; Rubén listened and said, "You will of course alert your bank and the credit card company, but is there nothing else you can add that might help identify him? He said nothing? You did not see his face?"

Chris shook his head.

"And you have no idea who might have done this to you?"

Chris paused, and the host and officer watched as troubled thoughts spun behind his eyes, but Chris shook his head slowly.

The officer spoke angrily in Spanish. The host nodded.

"What?" Chris said.

"It is shameful," Rubén said. "A mugging on the Camino. Unheard of!"

CHAPTER 20

Fault

Wearing a simple green jacket now, and a smaller bandage over his eye, Chris stood looking out the albergue lobby door, which he had propped open with his backpack. Behind him, at the lobby counter, Emilee attempted to hand her debit card to Rubén, the albergue host, who waved it away.

"Are you sure? Both nights?' Emilee said.

"I will not take it," Rubén said.

"But the jacket too. It is so kind of you. Did you hear that, Chris?"

Chris turned to look at the host, then turned and picked up his backpack and went out the door.

Chris and Emilee passed most of the day without conversation, and barely noticed the pleasant territory through which they walked. It was a fifty-kilometer stretch of relatively flat terrain—the valley of El Bierzo—sheltered by mountains all about, which had made for a temperate microclimate in the valley, rich with freshly picked vineyards and pink cherry orchards. But Chris and Emilee walked with their heads down most of the morning.

As the day progressed, Emilee attempted conversation, but received one-word answers for her trouble. She looked with concern at Chris, at the bandage above his eye, at his clenched jaw. As Villafranca del Bierzo came into view, the town where they would stay that night, she consulted the guidebook and said, "This poor town suffered the plague in 1589, a catastrophic flood in 1715, and war in the 1800s." Then she looked at him and quipped, "Sounds like just the place for us."

But he stared ahead woodenly.

The following morning, walking along the shoulder of the highway from Villafranca to Trabadelo, they fell into step with a couple about their age, Paul and Sherry, tall blond Lutherans from Minnesota, where Chris and Emilee had spent several happy years early in their marriage. Emilee enjoyed their company, laughing with them as they poked fun at their own Minnesota accents—"Ya sure, we are from Mini-soda, don't ya know. You betcha"—and swapped a few Minnesota winter jokes.

"What do Minnesotans do when the temperature hits thirty-two degrees? Have one last cookout before it gets cold."

"Minnesota: Come for the culture, stay because your car won't start."

Paul, attempting to draw Chris into the fun, said, "You'll like this one, Chris. How do you know you're from Minnesota? When you think it's a sport to gather food by drilling through ice and sitting there all day waiting for it to swim by."

After a long moment, Chris forced a smile with

hardly a glance at Paul, who looked down awkwardly.

Paul and Sherry walked on ahead a few minutes later, waving goodbye over their shoulders one more time.

When they were out of earshot, Emilee said, "It's not their fault, you know?"

Chris didn't answer.

"Well, do you know?" Emilee said.

"I know."

"It's not my fault either."

"I know."

"And it's not your fault."

Chris didn't respond for a few paces. Then he said quietly, "What if you had been with me? How could I have protected you, getting knocked out and all?"

Emilee's face softened.

They walked quietly for a few moments.

Chris' face hardened. "I think it was Gino."

"What?" Emilee said, shocked.

"Remember how strange he acted toward us when we saw him after the Cruz de Ferro? How he was sitting outside at that donation-only albergue with all the flags, out in the cold without his new coat on? I think his luck had turned."

Emilee pondered this.

Chris nodded slowly, bitterly. "It was Gino."

The trail left the highway and began to climb late in the day as the mountains of Galicia approached, the last ascent above 1,000 meters that they would encounter on the Camino. The hike was up a steep rocky path through a chestnut forest, but they did not make good time and entered a small town after dark. They entered its one albergue just in time to see a man with a dirty beard, shabby clothes, and hunched posture shuffle out of the lobby into the dormitory. Chris and Emilee placed their *credenciales* on the counter in front of the hostess, who frowned in the direction of the dormitory.

"I just gave our last bed to him," she said.

"Last bed? I thought the bed race was over for this year," Chris said.

"A bus brought a group of pilgrims this afternoon. Americans like you, on their way to meet a priest. If you have a tent, I will allow you to camp in our backyard since it is late. It is fenced."

Chris looked at Emilee, who shrugged. She didn't see any other options.

"Free?" Chris asked the hostess.

She shook her head. "Our facilities will be available to you, *señor*."

"Half-off?"

She shook her head.

Chris had been tempted to ditch the tent, which the Roncesvalles albergue host had given them, a couple times along the way because of the space it took up in his pack, but now he was glad he hadn't. It was easier to set up tonight than it had been in the Roncesvalles woods, due to the patio light and the flat grassy yard. The tight space inside the one-man tent required them to take turns crawling into their sleeping bags.

"It's going to be cold," Emilee said, pulling her bag close around her.

"Already is," Chris said.

"At least we're close to each other," Emilee said.

Chris lay there with his eyes open, his thoughts churning, imagining what he would say—and *do*—if he caught up to Gino. Or whoever it was who robbed him. But he couldn't shake the thought that it was Gino.

Emilee turned restlessly in her sleeping bag.

Footsteps approached outside the tent. "Excuse me," said a female voice.

Chris pulled open the tent flap and Emilee turned to look. It was the albergue hostess, bending over and looking in the tent.

"The homeless man left," she said. "There's no understanding those people. Perhaps one of you would like the bed?"

Chris looked at Emilee.

"You don't mind?" she said.

Chris shook his head.

Emilee slipped out of her sleeping bag, rolled it up, and carried it with her as she crawled out of the tent.

CHAPTER 21

Sarria

The hike up the remainder of the mountain the following day took them into Galicia, the last of the four "autonomous communities"—that is, regional governing authorities—that the Camino Francés passes through on its way to Santiago. The border of Galicia was marked by a colorful stone stele covered with well-meaning graffiti (these cement markers would continue the rest of the way to Santiago, counting down the kilometers). As they passed it, Emilee scratched her neck, then her cheek. "Did you get bit by mosquitoes?" she asked Chris.

"Not that I noticed."

"And you slept outside."

Emilee's eyes followed a group of seven or eight pilgrims walking some distance ahead of them in a loosely bunched line. She particularly noticed a short woman, about her age, with a lime-green backpack, turquoise bandana, and black denim capris. "Do any of those Americans look familiar to you?"

Chris looked at them a few moments and shook his head.

O Cebreiro was the first town they entered in Galicia, a mountaintop village of only 1,200, but it had played a role in Camino history out of proportion to its size. Here was born Don Elías Valiña Sampedro, the parish priest who spearheaded the resurgence of the Camino in the last decades of the twentieth century. He wrote the pilgrimage's first modern guidebook in 1982, lobbied authorities for its redevelopment, inspired the albergue system, and, with the help of his students, even painted the first yellow arrows pointing west. By 1989 Pope John Paul II had visited the Cathedral in Santiago, and by 1993 the entire Camino Francés had been designated a UNESCO World Heritage Site. Pilgrim societies sprang up, the tourist industry caught on, movies were made, books written—until more than 250,000 people per year were walking the Camino. It can all be traced to Father Elías, who dedicated thirty years of his life to restoring the ancient pathway. Chris and Emilee passed the church where he was laid to rest in O Cebreiro and the adjacent square where a bust of his head stands.

After O Cebreiro the route climbed to Alto de San Roque at 1,270 meters, dipped to the hamlet of Hospital de la Condesa, then rose swiftly again to Alto do Poio at 1,335 meters.

"This is the final high point of the Camino," Emilee said. "It's downhill, generally speaking, from here to Santiago."

The descent began abruptly, with a steep decline down a rocky trail the rest of that day to Triacastela, and continued the next day down to Sarria at 425 meters, a depth the Camino had not visited since Logroño some 500 kilometers ago. The walk to Sarria crossed small bridges and cut through chestnut and oak forests, a hike Emilee would have found delightful if not for the mosquito bites she had to keep scratching. As they approached Sarria in the late afternoon sun, the swollen red welts on her neck, cheek, and arms stood out.

"Still getting bit?" Chris asked.

"I wish you wouldn't remind me," Emilee said and scratched her neck again. "How come me and not you?"

"Because you're sweet. If I was a mosquito, I would definitely go for you and not me."

"Hmm," Emilee said, but she was glad to hear a bit of humor from him again. She only wished there were some other occasion for it.

Sarria was a small city, its population of 15,000 the greatest they would see until Santiago. They crossed another bridge to enter the heart of the city and passed a sign that greeted them in four languages:

Bienvenido   Welcome   Willkommen   Bienvenu

"A lot of pilgrims here," Chris said, noticing an unusual number of bright-eyed individuals with packs and staffs walking by the shop windows.

"That's because Sarria is just over 100 kilometers from Santiago," Emilee explained from the guidebook, "and the church will give you the official Compostela—the certificate of completion—for the whole pilgrimage if you just walk the last 100 kilometers, as long as you do it for spiritual reasons. So a lot of pilgrims come here to get started."

It was a typically handsome Spanish town: neat and narrow streets, sidewalk cafés under colorful awnings, and two- and three-story lofts with Juliet balconies above. Across one corner, Chris noticed a storefront with travel posters in the windows and a bilingual sign above the door:

Agencia de Viajes
Travel Agency

He eyed it moodily for several long seconds, unconsciously raising a finger to feel what was left of his bandage.

There were more than twenty albergues in Sarria, and Chris and Emilee did not stop at one until the edge of town, a two-story brick building surrounded on three sides by a patchy lawn, with long clotheslines that stretched from one corner of the building to a small copse of oaks. Chris' eyes fell on one of the pilgrims hanging laundry out to dry, a tall, powerfully built man in a clerical collar—it was the priest from Grand Rapids.

"It's Rambo the Priest," Chris said.

"What? Where?"

"Hanging clothes."

Chris crossed the lawn toward him. Emilee

followed.

The priest noticed them approaching. He wore the same bristly crew cut, and the rifle and bullets tattoos stuck out above his collar. After a moment's puzzlement, he recognized Chris.

"I was just thinking of you," Chris said.

The priest continued to hang his clothes. "You came. With your wife."

"Because of you," Chris said, and the accusatory note in his words caused the priest to look at him closely.

"You've lost a few pounds anyway," the priest said.

"Shouldn't you have reached Santiago by now?" Chris said.

"I did. But these"—he pointed to a group of people sitting at nearby picnic tables, eating Danishes— "though they gave up early, still want to get credit for walking the Camino. So they have played the tourist while I walked with the others, and I agreed to meet them here to walk the rest of the way."

Those at the tables waved and smiled at Chris and Emilee.

One of them raised his Danish and said with a smile, "*'The spirit is willing, but the flesh is weak,'* eh, Father?"

Another asked, "You from America?"

"Grand Rapids," Emilee said.

The woman with the lime-green backpack was sitting there, and she said to Emilee, "I thought I recognized you!"

"The Walmart toy aisle!" Emilee said.

"Yes. For my granddaughter," the woman said.

"Me too."

The woman stood and she and Emilee hugged.

Chris walked past them toward the lobby door.

The priest's eyes followed Chris.

CHAPTER 22

Odd Plans

In the morning light, Chris and Emilee exited the albergue just as the priest and his group were starting off on the path.

"Will we have to walk long before we take our first break, Father?" one of the men in his group said.

The priest noticed Chris and Emilee.

"Pete," he said, "you take the lead. Follow Pete, everyone." Pete was the hiker who had raised his Danish to the priest yesterday.

The priest let his group pass and fell in beside Chris. They nodded good-morning to each other. Emilee caught up with Donna (the woman with the lime-green backpack). The route out of Sarria crossed the Río Celerio on an arched Romanesque bridge and entered an oak forest.

"So our meeting at the travel agency was a divine appointment?" the priest said.

Chris gave him a sidelong look, then said, "We spent most of the first half of our walk completely exhausted, from the bed race and all. I developed a blister Job would have been proud of and spent a week in the hospital, running up a bill we can't pay. My pastor called me with a report from home—that our car was stolen. Which was bad enough, but the look of disappointment on my wife's face when I told her I'd let the insurance lapse was worse."

The priest looked at the cut and bruise over Chris' eye (Chris had removed the bandage).

"Yes, that was the crowning calamity, pardon the pun," Chris said. "I got hit over the head and mugged."

"Strange," the priest said. "Crime is practically unheard of on the Camino."

"You just heard of it." Chris clenched his jaw. "I think I know who did it. I hope I catch up to him. And if I do...."

"You know where he is?"

"I get the feeling he'll finish the Camino, no matter what, to get his slate wiped clean." Chris looked at the priest. "Bet he couldn't have done it to you."

They walked with the priest's group throughout the morning, passing several small towns, until they reached the 100 kilometer marker beside the path, an upright stone slab declaring in red paint: K. 100. Scores of scribbles left by pilgrims over the years covered the remainder of the slab. The priest's group clapped at the sight of the marker.

Pete turned and smiled at the priest. "I think we can make it, Father," he said.

The priest nodded and sighed at the same time.

Pete laughed and turned back around.

"How did a small group of pacifist fishermen ever win the Roman Empire to Christ?" the priest said. He looked pointedly at Chris. "The Almighty has some odd plans, doesn't he?"

Chris and the priest had passed Emilee and Donna, who had slowed while sharing grandchildren pictures with each other. They walked only a few feet in front of the women and overhead Emilee telling Donna about her mosquito bites. "For some reason I get them but not my husband," Emilee said.

"They look painful," Donna said.

"Ugly too," Emilee said. "I can't stop scratching them. But you haven't been bitten by any mosquitoes either?"

"No," Donna said.

"Anyone in your group complained?" Emilee asked.

"No. Is it even the season for them?"

At this the priest looked over his shoulder at Emilee, at the bumps on her neck and cheeks. "Can I take a look at those?" he said.

"I guess," Emilee said.

They stopped, and the priest looked at the red spots.

Emilee was embarrassed. "I can't stop scratching them. Seems I have new ones every morning."

"I hate to say this, Mrs. Danielson, but those may be bed bug bites," the priest said.

Emilee looked horrified. Everyone in the priest's group stopped and gathered around.

"What are you talking about?" Chris said angrily.

"I can't be sure," the priest said. "Bed bug bites and mosquito bites look alike. And bed bugs are rare on the

Camino. Albergues fumigate regularly. But since no one else has been bit…."

Emilee combed her fingers through her hair, looking for any sign of the bugs, and brushed at the sleeves and shoulders of her coat. "How can I know?"

"Bed bugs don't reside *on* people like lice," the priest said. "They sneak out at night, get their meal of blood from the victim, then go back in hiding."

"Then these can't be from bed bugs, because I get more each night."

"They don't reside on people, but they do hitchhike on people's things—on luggage, clothing, pieces of furniture. That's how they get around."

"Backpack!" She took her pack off, dropped it, and began to check it. Chris helped. "What am I looking for?" Emilee said.

"The bugs themselves," the priest said. "Tiny, reddish-brown. Or their fecal spots, shed skins, eggs."

"Ew," Emilee said, disgusted. She opened the backpack and started removing items.

"Have you had any red smears on the clothes you sleep in?"

"Not that I've noticed. Why?"

"If you rolled over and crushed one engorged with blood," the priest explained.

"No, I—Ohhh!" she moaned and held up her sleeping bag at arm's length, seeing dark stains on the edge of the inside fabric.

The priest took it from her, opened it more, and ran

his long blunt forefinger in the seam between the nylon shell of the bag and the fabric interior. He removed his finger and on it were two of the oval, wingless parasites, red with blood. At the sight, the others took a step back.

Emilee moaned. "What do I do?"

The priest flicked the bugs into a bush. "Best to get all new gear and clothes. The bumps will clear up when the bites stop. They're not dangerous, just a nuisance. You should tell the albergues you slept in since the bites started, and what bunk you used if you recall."

"The homeless guy!" Chris said.

"What?" the priest said.

"That's when they started, Em—after the hostess gave you the homeless guy's bed."

Emilee could not stop the tears. "Chris, can you believe it?"

"Why did I do this to you? Let's head back to Sarria," Chris said.

CHAPTER 23

Are You Ready to Go Home?

Before they headed back to Sarria, everyone moved off the trail, and the women in the priest's group picked through their packs for articles of clothing for Emilee. They handed them to Donna, who carried them to Chris, who gave them to Emilee behind a clump of bushes.

Chris and Emilee walked back toward Sarria with shoulders slumped. Instead of her jacket, Emilee wore a sweatshirt under a windbreaker. Her pants were too big. Nothing matched. She had her walking stick but no backpack, just a small bag with a few items in it.

In Sarria they got a hotel room, where Chris left Emilee to clean up while he returned to the albergue they had stayed in last night and told the host about the bed bugs and pointed out the bed Emilee had slept in. The host was none-too-pleased. Then Chris stepped outside and called the albergue in Triacastela, where they had stayed the night before, and described to the host, the best he could over the phone, where Emilee had slept. The guidebook also had the phone number for the albergue where the hostess had given Emilee the bed the homeless man had vacated. He told the hostess he was sure that was where Emilee had picked up the bed bugs and told her she should not have given the bed to Emilee without changing the sheets. "I was just trying to be nice, *señor*," she said.

After the calls, Chris walked down the street toward the hotel.

"Hey! Chris, Chris!"

He turned to see who was calling him. It was Pete, from the priest's group, jogging after him.

"I'm glad I caught you," Pete said when he reached Chris. "They told me at the albergue you were walking this way."

"We're staying at that hotel." Chris pointed down the street.

"Good for you. How's Emilee?"

"Upset. What are you doing here? How did you get here?"

"I got a ride." Pete looked around, took a roll of euros out of his pocket, and handed them to Chris. "We took a collection—Father's idea. He says to use this to resupply Emilee or take a rest or whatever you need. It's yours."

Chris thumbed through the roll. "There are several hundred—" He looked up at Pete. "Wow."

"I better get back," Pete said. "My ride's waiting. I *am* supposed to walk the last 100 kilometers." He turned and jogged away.

Chris called after him: "Thanks, Pete. I mean, everyone."

Pete waved over his shoulder.

Dumbstruck, Chris thumbed through the money roll again, then slipped it in his pocket. He stood looking at the hotel for a moment, then took out his phone and dialed.

"Pastor Tyler here."

"Hi, Pastor. Chris Danielson."

"Hi, Chris. I've been meaning to give you a call, but no news about your car. No other problems at your house, though."

"That's a relief. Thanks again for checking in on it. I really shouldn't have dumped that on you."

"How's the pilgrimage?"

"Not so good, really. I'll spare you the details. The reason I called, I'll take the Family Ministry position. It seems like God—"

"Well, Chris, that's another reason I was going to call you. The personnel committee didn't think you and Emilee were really interested in it."

"No, no. We are."

"Well, they didn't think it was your passion."

Chris did not know what to say to that.

"I believe you met Clem and Jeannie Wagner, the Christian counselors who joined our church in the spring? The committee has been talking to them for a few weeks now about the Family Ministry position."

"I don't like the way this conversation is going, Tyler."

"I'll just be straightforward with you, Chris. The committee wants to hire them."

Chris slumped down on a nearby bus stop bench.

"Chris? You there?"

Chris closed his eyes. "Yes. What about you, Tyler? You want to hire them too?"

"I do. Marriage counseling is their expertise. They seem a perfect fit."

After Chris hung up, he sat bent over on the bench for a few minutes. As he was about to rise, he noticed the travel agency that had caught his attention when they passed through town yesterday. He stood and walked toward it instead of the hotel.

He entered their hotel room a half hour later, carrying an envelope from the travel agency. Emilee came out of the bathroom wearing a robe and with a hotel towel wrapped around her wet hair. The bites were visible on her neck and cheek. Her eyes were red from crying.

"This was a mistake," Chris said. "Are you ready to go home?"

"Chris, I've had bugs crawling on me at night."

Emilee looked more like herself the next morning as they stood in front of the Estación de Autobuses in Sarria, waiting for the bus. Her bag and Chris' backpack rested on the ground beside them. There was relief in her eyes and a small smile on her lips.

"It's an hour's ride to Coruña, then a nonstop flight

to Heathrow," Chris said. "Dana will be there to meet the plane, and I put in a special request—demand—for Riley and Quinner too."

Emilee's smile grew.

The bus pulled up, air brakes hissing. A few passengers stepped off, and the driver collected their luggage for them. Then he reached for Emilee's bag.

"That's okay," she said. "This is all I have. I'll just carry it on."

He reached for Chris' pack, but Chris waved him off. "I'm not going."

The driver climbed back onboard. "We are ready to depart, *señora*."

Emilee stared at Chris. "What do you mean you're not going?"

"I'm going to finish this thing, but I'm not going to put you through it anymore." He handed Emilee the travel agency envelope. "There's just one ticket in there, nonrefundable."

"I'm not going without you." She tried to hand the envelope back to Chris, but he wouldn't take it.

"I bought it with the priest's money," he said. "It's nonrefundable. You'll be throwing away their money if you don't go."

Emilee looked at the envelope, at the bus, back at Chris. "What are you doing to me?" she said.

"*Señora, por favor*," the bus driver said.

"I called Tyler. He gave the Family Ministry job to someone else."

"Oh Chris."

Chris clenched his jaw. "I'm finishing this."

Emilee considered the hard look on his face, and said angrily, "To find God's will, or find Gino?"

Chris didn't answer.

"It is time," the bus driver said.

"Emilee, Dana will be there. The girls will be there," Chris said.

"We have to go, *señora*."

"It's nonrefundable, and it's not our money," Chris said.

Crying, Emilee shook her head at him. "Oh, you big—" She turned away and climbed the bus steps.

Chris watched until she took a seat and the bus began to pull out. As it did, a woman rolled down her window and told Chris off in Spanish.

CHAPTER 24

The Three Spires

Between Sarria and Santiago, four complete stages of the Camino Francés remain, four full days of walking. Chris was determined to make it in three. If his blister opened up again, it opened up again.

He first retraced his steps to the 100 kilometer marker and then, just beyond the marker, to the point in the path where Emilee had learned she carried bed bugs. His eyes welled as he recalled her anguish and humiliation. *Why did I do this to her?* He paid little attention to the towns he passed through, some too small to register population counts in the guidebook; though he did take note of Portomarín with its strange sight of ancient ruins, including a Roman bridge, standing in the middle of a flowing river. When he reached Hospital Alta da Cruz, the guidebook's suggested stage stop for the day, he kept walking into the night—in pitch-darkness between the rural towns. He kept walking until his legs felt like rubber, and finally turned in at a little six-bed albergue in Eirexe. He had walked forty-seven kilometers since leaving Emilee on the bus that morning.

He walked farther the next day, blowing through Melide, which was another suggested stage stop, in the early afternoon. The rain began to fall, and it would continue intermittently the rest of the way to Santiago, because despite Professor Henry Higgins' claim to the contrary in *My Fair Lady*, the rain in Spain does *not* fall mainly on the plain, but in Galicia. As Chris followed a gravel and dirt path along a highway, he took out his poncho—the poncho Gino had encouraged him to buy—and pulled it over his shoulders and pack. Cars and trucks rumbled by, wipers swishing. Chris kept up his pace and gained on other pilgrims.

He came to Arzúa, a town of about 6,000, at twilight, where he should have stopped. Here were plenty of albergues, drugstores with ointment for his burning heel, and good cell coverage for a call to Emilee—if she would talk to him. But he kept walking, in the rain, in the dark, for hours the only human being on the trail. He reached Arca at midnight, woke the hostess in the first albergue he saw, and fell fully clothed on the bunk she gave him. He had covered three Camino stages in two days.

That left only twenty kilometers to Santiago the next day. Shaky and weak, for he had only picked at chip bags and convenience store sandwiches the last couple of days, he ate a quick breakfast and rejoined the route. It followed the main road through Arca, turning right at the town hall—and up ahead he saw Pete and others from the priest's group sitting at tables at a sidewalk café. He crossed to the other side of the street before they had a chance to see him, feeling ashamed of himself for avoiding these people who had been so kind to them—but he had to keep walking.

The morning was bright and beautiful, and as the earthen trail wound through a shade-dappled eucalyptus forest, he thought, with a pang of loss, how much he and Emilee would have enjoyed this final leg of the Camino if their plan had worked out. He remembered, as though from another life, his original purpose for this trip: *We won't rush, won't over-plan, but just walk and pray and maybe journal and ask God to speak to us.* But those good intentions, those lofty goals, had come to nothing. He knew he was no longer walking as a pilgrim.

The rain began to fall heavily again at Lavacolla, a hamlet ten kilometers from Santiago. Chris followed an elderly couple onto a bridge that crossed a stream just past the hamlet.

"Would you look there?" the woman said in an English accent and pointed at two pilgrims in brown habits washing themselves in the stream in the rain. "Have they lost their wits?"

"I read about that, my dear," the man answered. "Lavacolla, the town's name, literally means, 'Wash private parts.' Medieval pilgrims—not fond of bathing, you know—stopped here to wash up before continuing to the cathedral. Out of respect for the Apostle. I suppose the monks are following suit."

"Excuse me," Chris said, stepping around the couple on the bridge and continuing on.

Five kilometers later, now on a paved road, he climbed to the top of a hill where a group of pilgrims had stopped to point and clap. Two of the pilgrims sat on bikes.

"What is it?" Chris said.

"The city of Santiago," one of the bicyclists said. Chris saw, below the hill, the suburbs and city of 180,000 spread out before them under a gray sky. "And there"—the bicyclist pointed—"the three spires of the cathedral, our destination. See them?"

Chris could just make out the spire-tops above the hazy skyline.

"This is the first place the cathedral can be seen on the Camino," said another pilgrim, a walker, "which is why this hill is called Monte do Gozo in the local language, which means Hill of Joy. Just another hour or two." He beamed at Chris.

Chris forced an awkward smile and continued down the hill to the city.

CHAPTER 25

A Flash of Blue

The pilgrim route to Old Town Santiago passes through the modern suburb of San Lázaro, follows Rúa dos Concheiros (named for the street venders who hawked seashells to pilgrims in medieval days), and enters the historic city center on Rúa das Casas Reais (named for the kings who were crowned at the cathedral).

As a light rain fell, Chris walked with many pilgrims through the Old City. They made their way down the very middle of a granite-slabbed street, for pedestrians—incoming pilgrims and tourists—are the preferred traffic in the historic quarter. They passed *tapas* bars, memento shops, kiosks, side alleys, cafés and bars. High, balconied buildings of gray and brown brick rose above them like canyon walls.

Most of them walked with beaming faces, eyes cast ahead for the cathedral. Chris walked with his eyes searching faces—at the sidewalk tables, the shop windows, in the crowded street. He scarcely heard the excited chatter around him.

The chatter increased as the street opened onto a wide stone courtyard, on the other side of which was the archway—a long tunnel under buildings—that led to the cathedral. Anticipation built around him as the pilgrims entered the tunnel, which reverberated with lively noise—bagpipes playing, conversations and laughter, the echo of a hundred bootsteps.

More pilgrims were exiting the tunnel, however, than entering it—that is, walking in the opposite direction of Chris and the others—for the noon Pilgrim Mass had just dismissed, and for a moment the tunnel resembled an airport terminal at Christmas, in which a flash of electron blue, among the bodies going the other way, barely registered on Chris' consciousness, though a frown came to his face.

"The last stamp in the *credencial*," called someone else in the tunnel, "let's go get our *Compostela*!"

Chris emerged from the tunnel onto the Praza do Obradoiro, the great stone plaza of several acres breadth that fronts the cathedral. Scores of pilgrims stood on the plaza gazing with awe at the towering cathedral façade twenty-four stories high, the great glazed windows, and, atop the middle steeple, the statue of Saint James in pilgrim attire—hat, cape, and staff. They raised their phones for photos, wiped away tears, and laughed joyously as they migrated to the middle of the plaza for a better view.

But Chris hardly raised his eyes. He stopped and looked back at the tunnel as the screen of his mind replayed the image: a flash of an electron blue jacket in the press of bodies exiting the tunnel.

Clenching his teeth, he headed back into the tunnel, which had largely emptied, and hurried through it to emerge in the wide stone courtyard on the other side.

He slowed to look among the pilgrims lingering there, but saw no blue jacket, and cast his gaze down the long street he had walked only minutes ago, where now the throng of pilgrims headed away from the cathedral. *Come on, come on—at least help me with this.* In a momentary parting in the crowd he saw his electron blue jacket, worn by a tall man—obviously Gino—with the hood over his head against the drizzle, and Chris set off across the courtyard after him.

He trotted until, reaching the street, he lost sight of Gino in the crowd, and slowed to try to spot the blue jacket again, watching carefully, because some pilgrims were turning off into side streets and shops.

He caught up with the bulk of the throng and, after a moment, saw the blue hood pop up, as though floating on the wave of the crowd, about forty feet ahead. Then the blue hood turned slowly, angled toward one side of the crowd, and dipped out of sight.

Chris veered in that direction, waited for the crowd to clear—and saw him! He sat with his back to Chris, head down, shoulders hunched, on a block wall that bordered a landscape island in the street. Chris hesitated one moment—*Is it really him?*—until he saw the rip in the lower back of the jacket, and he remembered that moment burned on his mind: the *crack* of a staff upon his head, the painful explosion above his right eye, and the *rip* of his jacket upon a rock as he fell to the ground and lost consciousness.

He took a deep angry breath and strode up behind

Gino. "Hey!" he said and grabbed him by the shoulder and spun him to his feet—but it wasn't Gino. It was a thin-faced old man who almost stumbled over the block wall even as he threw up an arm to ward off expected blows and shrank back.

"*Por favor,* no, no!"

Chris was too stunned to speak. The man before him had watery eyes, a gray-stubbled face, and flecks of dried spit on his lips. The hood had fallen away to reveal a scabby bald head.

"*Por favor,* no."

"What are you doing in my jacket?"

Several people had stopped to stare and a Santiago police officer, in a dark blue uniform with a gold badge on the right breast and "POLICÍA" on the left, approached.

"What is the problem?" the officer said. "Miguel, are you bothering this gentleman?"

"He's wearing my jacket," Chris said.

"No, no, he gave it to me," the old man—Miguel—said.

"You gave it to him, *señor*?" the police officer asked Chris.

"No."

"The tall Italian," Miguel said. "On the cold night—or I would have frozen."

Chris was taken aback by these words. He noticed that Miguel wore only sandals with threadbare socks, damp from the rain. Some of the anger in his tense muscles and face drained away. "He stole it from me," he said quietly.

"Miguel?" the police officer said.

"The Italian," Chris said.

"Can you prove it's your jacket, *señor*?"

"I wrote my name on the tag."

The officer turned Miguel around, rolled back the hood and collar, and read the tag. "Give it to him, Miguel," he said.

Miguel, mumbling to himself, had slipped a shaky hand into a front jacket pocket as the officer examined the tag; now he tried to sneak it out, but a wallet and a wad of euros fell to the pavement.

"Miguel!" the officer scolded. "Is that yours too, *señor*?"

"It looks like my wallet. It had €300 in it."

The officer picked up the wallet and cash. He handed the wallet to Chris, who opened it to see that it was empty—of cash, ID cards, bank and credit cards. The officer counted the bills. "I get €241," he said with a frown at Miguel.

"I purchased a room outside the quarter. That is all," Miguel said.

The officer handed the bills to Chris, who slipped them in the wallet. Slowly, with some effort, Miguel took off the coat and gave it to Chris. The officer walked away. Miguel sat on the block wall, head down, mumbling to himself.

Confused and irritated, Chris looked at him, then

said, "Why did he give you the money?"

Miguel continued to mumble, head down.

"I couldn't trace the money, track it down like the coat. Why'd he give it to you?"

Miguel didn't answer. He seemed to be crying a little, though his watery eyes made it hard to tell. He crossed his arms and rubbed his shoulders for warmth. "A room outside the quarter. That is all. No *vino*."

Chris looked at the coat in his hand, let out a loud breath, and put the coat on Miguel's lap—who flinched, gawking at it.

Chris opened the wallet and removed two €20 notes and started to hand them to Miguel, but paused and, with a frown, instead placed the whole wallet with all the cash on Miguel's lap, and kept only the two €20 notes for himself. He slipped them in his pocket, turned, and started to walk away.

"*Señor?*"

Chris stopped and turned.

"He kept the book, though. He came back later and asked me for it—*el Testamento*, in your pocket. He said he was reading it."

Chris stared for some moments at Miguel at these words, more of the tightness in his shoulders and face melting away.

When he started to turn away, Miguel spoke again. "And indeed I have seen him doing so. Twice."

Chris' jaw hardened again. "Where?"

CHAPTER 26

Second Thoughts

Chris retraced his steps through Old Town until he spotted the *tapas* bar Miguel had described. He approached it warily, scanning the parties at the wrought iron tables on the sidewalk patio, each table under its own umbrella. No sign of Gino. A row of old wine barrels separated the patio from the interior. Chris walked past the barrels, entered the dining room—which smelled of wine, fried peppers, and green olives—and scanned the tables and bar. No sign of Gino.

"Can I help you, *señor*?" the hostess asked.

Chris shook his head, frowned, and walked back outside. He stood looking up and down the street for a moment, noticed the café on the other side, crossed to it, and requested a table by the window. The waiter kept insisting so Chris ordered a plate of *chopitos*, which are battered and fried baby squid—"It is our specialty, *señor*, and you look famished"—to go with his coffee, and sat with his elbows on the table watching the *tapas* bar through the window.

He paid it close attention until a woman of perhaps forty years walked by in the street in the continuing drizzle, in the direction of the cathedral. She walked alone, her backpack seeming too much for her thin frame, her hair streaking gray. She wasn't Melanie, the hotel keeper in Saint-Jean-Pied-de-Port, but the hope that lit her face reminded him of the look on Melanie's face when she drove them to the pilgrims' office that morning in her jeep.

"He listened to la musique de Dieu all night long," *Melanie said, looking over her shoulder, taking her* *hands off the wheel, pressing them together in a* *gesture of prayer. "Always a disciple of Voltaire, but* *le Notre Père, le Notre Père."*

And what had Emilee said as they climbed the mountain later that morning?

"Le Notre Père," *she said between breaths, "that* *French phrase Melanie kept repeating in the jeep—the* *guy in the office said it means The Lord's Prayer. She* *was telling us her husband was praying it while* *listening to the music."*

In other words, she was telling them that her husband, dying of cancer, had turned from doubt to faith through the music she had played for him, music from their old radio station—music he wouldn't have heard if Chris and Emilee had not come on pilgrimage, had not arrived late in Saint Jean, had not been given a stinky room. Chris wondered that he had not given this wonderful occurrence a second thought.

The rain poured outside the café window as the waiter from the next shift filled Chris' cup and cleared away the *chopitos* plate. A young Korean couple dashed by Chris' window, ducked inside the café, and, laughing as they brushed raindrops off each other, sat at a table near Chris. They took out their colorfully stamped *credenciales* and official *Compostelas* and admired them on the table. The man said something in Korean and the woman answered in English, "We'll bring them when they're older."

They brought Nick and Louise to Chris' mind.

"And already he is tired of me." Louise's big dark eyes flashed.

"Louise!" Nick said. Then, with a pleading look at Chris and Emilee: "It is not so."

Chris remembered walking with them on the trail, as they fought openly about their sex life, until words of separation came up—and Emilee separated them, and walked calmingly by Louise as he walked ahead with Nick.

Then in the crowded dining room of the albergue in Burgos:

"She's going to leave me," Nick said frantically as he approached their table. "She told me to find a marriage counselor or she's leaving. You are old and married. Will you come and talk to us?"

Then in their hotel room Chris and Emilee felt powerless to say anything to help the young couple, and sat there shell-shocked as they yelled at each other.

"We need to get out of here," Chris whispered when Nick and Louise stepped out for a moment.

"This is a disaster," Emilee said.

"Let's just read some Scripture—do something

spiritual—and leave."

And so, when they returned to the room, he read: "at the beginning the Creator made them male and female ... For this reason a man will leave his father and mother and be united to his wife ... they are no longer two, but one."

When he looked up from the page, Nick and Louise were both crying and gazing softly at each other.

"I am sorry, Nicky."

"I will never walk away, Louise."

The rain had stopped and night fallen by the time Chris left the café, crossed the street, and entered the *tapas* bar again. There was no sign of Gino, of course, but Chris felt no frustration.

... chasing the thief through the woods, through thick trees and bushes. He rushed to his backpack, dropped by a bush, and bent to pick it up ...

—a fearful cry, and the blow cracked down on his head.

—a fearful cry (the same cry heard again, but somehow Chris recognized pain in it this time), and the blow cracked down on his head.

—a fearful cry (the same cry once more, and Chris recognized the pain as sorrow), and the blow cracked down on his head ...

"The tall Italian gave it to me. On the cold night or I would have frozen. He kept the book, though—he was reading it."

CHAPTER 27

Laying It Down

The next morning, after a long night's sleep and his best in many days, Chris walked once again down the Old Town streets toward the cathedral. Yesterday's rain had left the sky above the city blue and sparkling.

He passed a shop where a six-foot-high scallop shell, made of cardboard, stood outside the open door, and he remembered what the German father had said about the symbolism of the shell: *"The lines represent the fingers of an open hand, the generosity of pilgrims and those who would aid them."* And a new string of memories flitted through his mind: the pilgrims stepping out of line at the fountain in the mountains to let Chris and Emilee drink before them, the albergue host bringing them a tent and sandwiches that first night in Roncesvalles, the young men getting under Chris' arms and practically carrying him and his blister to León, Pete running to him with a roll of euros....

Today as he entered the tunneled archway leading to the cathedral grounds, he enjoyed the sights and sounds of the happy pilgrims around him, and the bagpipe music—a traditional Galician sound—echoing off the stone walls.

He exited the archway and walked into the middle of the Praza do Obradoiro with the other pilgrims, and today he admired the majestic cathedral façade with them. Nearby, a school group in uniforms listened as their teacher pointed at the cathedral and instructed them in Spanish. Just in front of Chris, a woman with a Cajun drawl showed her husband a copper coin. "That's the cathedral on their coin," she said. "See the likeness?"

"Ah!" he said.

"Grandpa! Grandpa! Grandpa!"

Chris turned and saw Riley and Quinner running to him across the plaza stones, with Emilee, Dana, and Michael walking up behind them. Chris, his heart thrilled, fell to a knee and scooped the little girls to him in a big hug, one to an arm, laughing and kissing their foreheads.

"What is this? What are you doing here?" He addressed the question to Riley and Quinner but looked up at Emilee, who approached with eyes full of emotion.

"We've come to gratuate you," Riley said.

"Our grampa walked this many miles," Quinner said. She held up one hand with all five fingers extended, closed it, opened it, closed it, opened it....

Chris laughed, reluctantly released them, and stood. "Dana and Michael?" he said.

"Congratulations, Dad," Dana said.

"You've dropped 20 pounds!" Michael said.

Chris laughed again and patted his stomach. "I always knew there were abs in there somewhere." He looked hesitantly at Emilee, who smiled at him—to his relief. He embraced her tightly, kissed her. Kissed her again.

She leaned her head back to look at him. "You okay?" she said.

"Wonderful. I've been a knucklehead, honey."

She nodded readily. Dana and Michael laughed. And Chris.

"I never found Gino, but I found my coat and money on a guy who needed it. And Gino found what he needed."

"I'm not sure I understand all that but it's good?" Emilee said.

He nodded, looked deeply in her eyes. "He's always had a plan for us, Emilee, used us. And taken care of us."

She nodded and smiled softly. "I know that, honey."

"Mom promised us some sightseeing, Dad," Dana said.

"I'd like to see this Finisterre on the edge of the Atlantic coast," Michael said. "The name means 'End of the Earth'—the Romans named it."

"And we're not far from Portugal. We rented a car," Dana said.

"Sure," Chris said, "would love to. But there's one more stop I want to make to complete my pilgrimage, a return to one of the sites. Don't worry, we can drive. Couple hours."

"Grandpa, is that the church you walked to? It's a lot bigger than ours," Riley said.

Chris looked at the stone steps leading up to the cathedral, lined with pilgrims waiting to enter. "Want to go inside? After all, I did walk 500 miles to get here. Then we'll hit the road."

They stayed longer in the cathedral than intended, for they had a chance to witness the *botafumeiro* (literally, "smoke-belcher") in action. It is the world's largest censer, a 175-pound incense burner, resembling a large lantern, that sweeps in an arc over the worshipers' heads as the choir sings and the organ plays, diffusing light gray fragrant smoke in its wake. "They say it was originally installed to cover up the smell of all those medieval pilgrims showing up at church," Chris whispered to Michael. The girls watched in awe as eight men in red robes yanked ropes attached to a pulley system above the altar, swinging the censer higher and faster. "It can reach fifty miles per hour," Chris said.

Then they climbed in the white Nissan X-Trail SUV and Chris gave Michael directions. They zoomed past fields and woodlands turning golden brown, covering in minutes ground that had taken days to walk. Chris watched it pass from the passenger seat, turning often to laugh and chat with Emilee and the girls.

Michael parked in the dirt lot opposite the Cruz de Ferro, next to a campervan. After they crossed the road, Riley trotted toward the mound of stone, Quinner following. "Try to find a long, flat one," Chris called.

"Okay, Grandpa," Riley said.

Emilee, Dana, and Michael helped the little girls pick through the loose stones scattered around the base of the mound while Chris stopped to look up at the iron cross on top of the wooden pole.

"Here's a pretty one, Grandpa, and it's as big as your hand." Riley brought him a flat white stone.

"That works."

Chris took the stone. The family gathered around. He took out his black Sharpie and, as everyone watched, wrote on the stone in big bold letters: "Jesus Paid It All." He looked at the words a long moment, then at Emilee, who nodded at him.

He took her hand and they began to climb the mound, but Chris stopped and turned. "Can we all go?" he said.

Dana and Michael nodded, took Riley's and Quinner's hands, and climbed the mound with Chris and Emilee.

When they reach the wooden pole, Riley and Quinner stared at all the bright mementos attached to it. Chris looked at Emilee, who took one side of the stone in her hand, and together they bent and placed the stone at the foot of the pole. They straightened, and Chris looked up at the cross one more time, peace on his face.

He took Emilee's hand and the family descended the mound.

HEY THERE, READERS!

Thanks for reading our book—what a privilege to be able to share our hearts with you!

We are indie authors—that is, we have no big corporate bucks backing us, but rely on satisfied readers to spread the word. So if you enjoyed *Burden Stone,* **please recommend us to your friends via social media.** And if you get a chance, **please leave us a review on *Burden Stone's* Amazon page**. Much appreciated!

Want to know more about the real Chris and Emilee? Have a question about the Camino? **Connect with us on Facebook**:

www.facebook.com/BurdenStoneNovel

ABOUT THE AUTHORS

Once a devout atheist, **William Ray** became a Christian through a personal experience with Jesus Christ. After serving as a pastor for 25 years, mostly in the Phoenix area, William retired (early) to pursue writing projects, serve in a jail ministry, and oversee his sermon illustration service for pastors, illustrationsforsermons.com. In addition to *Burden Stone,* William is the author of *Answered Prayer: The Jesus Plan*, the light-hearted reference book *The 100 Most Entertaining Predictions about the 21st Century*, and the practical reference book *Bible Sidekick: Study Helps for Believers New and Old*. William holds the Master of Divinity degree from Southwestern Baptist Theological Seminary and an English degree from Grand Canyon University. William and his wife Lynette have been married for 34 years and have two lovely daughters and two absolutely beautiful granddaughters.

Contact information: billray@joyinthedesert.com

Chris Danielson is an author, film maker, and conference speaker. He has spent over 30 years in radio, including the last 15 years alongside his wife in "The Chris and Emilee Show." In addition to *Burden Stone,* Chris is the author of *Bible Sidekick: Study Helps for Believers New and Old* and writer and director of the engaging documentary *Bible Idiots*, in which he also appears. Chris' passion is creatively teaching the Scriptures, which he has done as a pastor, a missionary, and a stand-up comic. Chris also loves sports (for which he has served as an on-air host); but if not enjoying football, hockey, or NASCAR, you'll find him with his granddaughters Riley and Quinn (and probably giving them whatever they want).

Contact information: chris@bibmediagroup.com

Made in the USA
Middletown, DE
18 August 2018